1961

The Rise
of Father Roland

The Rise
of Father Roland

A NOVEL BY

Rev. William L. Doty

THE BRUCE PUBLISHING COMPANY
MILWAUKEE

To My Aunts

The Rise
of Father Roland

CHAPTER I

My MEMORIES of the seminary are clear in many ways, confused in others. By confused, I mean that the years seem to run together in my mind. I find it hard to remember if a particular event happened in Second Philosophy or Second Theology, but the events themselves stand out clearly regardless of the time when they occurred. Likewise my general impressions, over-all, have not been blunted by time. I have always characterized my years there as a sort of purgatory on earth with all the qualities that purgatory implies: pain, yet pain willingly accepted; confidence of final happiness, yet confidence badly tainted with impatience; joy in the assurance that God was near, yet vexation that God was not near enough and might not become so for a longer time than one expected. I have heard other priests speak wistfully of the seminary years as the happiest period of their lives. I cannot agree. Some have even said they would like to live the time over again. I can only shudder at the thought; I cannot understand why anyone should want to make a transitional stage permanent.

I do not mean to imply that my days in the seminary were not days of many graces, and of great growth spiritually and mentally. How could I say this? It was there that I first knew

1

the happiness of exploring dogma, scripture, and the rest — a fresh happiness of the mind which I have never been able to regain in the same form. It was in the seminary that I first began to realize the meaning of contemplation, the joy of personal, experiential union with God — but I will not burden this account with details of my spiritual life, such as it is, or was. I can only shamefully confess that in the seminary I was, for a time at least, convinced that I would be a saint, and that now, after more than thirty years in the priesthood, I feel less close to attaining this ideal than I felt then.

But apart from generalities, I think I can remember every incident of even a slightly unusual nature which occurred in the six seemingly endless years of my preparation for the priesthood. Of course I recall my first day when everything seemed so much different from what I had expected. Imagine the seminarians gathered during recreation at the handball court singing the latest hit tunes! I think this was a great shock to an impressionable young man who, while not puritanical, had envisioned a seminary world of pious phrases and endless beads slipping reverently through innocent fingers. The reality, as I soon discovered, was entirely different from, but, on the whole, better than my expectations.

I remember vividly too the first examinations, the first faculty appraisal, so damaging to my vanity, the holidays, the reception of orders of various degrees, the unexpected departure of seemingly saintly classmates, and other events of this type. Other incidents, often very trivial, also remain in memory, such as the time our Homiletics professor inadvertently appeared in class without his toupee. Somehow in an enclosed environment, trivial things often seem either extraordinarily serious or amazingly funny. I know that laughter or worry came easily then about things that would now hardly impress me at all.

I could, I think, make an endless list of seminary memories,

2

but there is one event which overshadows them all, not necessarily in importance but in the impression which it made on me. I am not referring here to my ordination to the priesthood. That stands alone in a separate compartment of my mind. I am referring to the fire which caused two men's deaths, changed the lives of at least two others, and branded the emotions of scores of young men with a terror that, in my case at least, the years have been unable to erase.

The evening began innocently enough. During recreation period the annual "Gaudeamus" was presented at the hand-ball courts, which served as a sort of outdoor theater for all our attempts at organized entertainment. My friend, Willoughby, was the chief comedian and did an excellent job, judging by the laughter and shouts of approval which he received from those of us who were spectators. He did an imitation of the Homiletics professor which could only be described as classical; for he did not neglect to introduce a toupee into the act. Needless to say, the toupee was made to fall off several times, each fall bringing delighted howls from all present. The finale of Willoughby's little act involved his attempt to balance a valise on his shoulder. This puzzled the audience for a while until he looked up owlishly and said, "I'm just trying to get a grip on myself." Seminarians laugh at almost anything. Their response to this little pun was intemperate.

I mention all this because the happy spirit in which we entered the chapel for night prayers contrasts so strikingly with the atmosphere which enveloped us all just a few hours later.

I did, however, have what might now be described as a sense of foreboding as the night prayers proceeded, although at the time I considered it merely the nervous unease that I often experienced at night shortly before bed. I was restless during the litany and a vague sort of fear gripped my heart, causing me to shift from knee to knee and to look here and there in the chapel, with little or no concentration on lifting my mind and heart to God. In our seminary, as in most, I believe, the choir stalls for the students face toward the center aisle and thus I was able without any difficulty to see the countenances of the men on the opposite side. As I glanced carelessly from one to another, I saw nothing to fix my attention until my gaze settled on the protagonist of our evening's entertainment, Willoughby.

He was kneeling absolutely straight, which was not in itself unusual, but his head was thrown back at a most peculiar angle so that his eyes seemed fixed on the ceiling almost directly above his head. This was strange procedure but it would not, I think, have troubled me overmuch had it not been for the wild look of exhilaration and almost of pride which seemed to flash from his eyes and in fact from his whole visage. In a word, he gave every appearance of being a perfect madman.

Let me say at once that seminarians have been known occasionally to become "rapt" in spiritual contemplation and to lose momentarily in the act of union with God the consciousness of their surroundings. Such ecstasies are, I presume, rare, at least in open chapel but I am confident that, privately, many a student for the priesthood has been caught up in such a way while at prayer. I myself have had touches of what we used to call "the glow" — an almost experiential knowledge of God's presence in and near one. Of course, this was many years ago. For a long time now, I have had to move forward by the dark — and often cold — light of faith.

Willoughby's face, however, had a sort of satanic look, certainly not an expression of gentle and holy spiritual joy. Suddenly he lowered his head and looked directly at me, and smiled pleasantly. Uneasily I avoided his eyes.

I thought no more about it at the time but tried to concentrate on the rest of the prayers. I even took a certain pleasure in the hymn, *Adoro Te Devote*, although I could not

4

enjoy my singing as much as I should have liked because Pawling, who sat next to me, always drowned everyone else out with his bellowing. I have always thought highly of Pawling; his only fault — if I can call it that — was that he was overfond of his own voice.

I remember going up to Father Higgins' room for a consultation after chapel. I had been bothered by the notion that I should be a missionary and, although the idea horrified me, I felt that I should seek counsel as to whether or not this was God's will for me.

I sat in the graying priest's wooden rocker and rocked back and forth as I explained my problem.

He was very serious but well balanced, I had always felt; and, looking back, I can say that his advice to me was usually helpful and sound. He listened respectfully until I had finished; then he asked one or two questions and at last gave me his advice.

"No," he said, wheezing slightly. He was afflicted with asthma. "Numerous seminarians get ideas of possible vocations to Trappist monasteries, the Jesuits, and the missionary orders. Some of them really seem to be called in this fashion by God. In your case, however, I think God is calling you to the diocesan priesthood. I don't think your temperament or your physical substratum equips you for the missionary life. This is no reflection on you; the best vocation for you is the one God wants you to embrace."

He spoke like this regularly. Terms like "physical substratum" were as natural to his lips as "damn" would be to a tired housewife.

I must admit that I was both relieved and hurt by his response — hurt because, despite his assurances, I felt that my lack of missionary qualities was an imperfection of considerable proportions.

In a melancholy frame of mind, I lumbered through the hall toward my own room. For the first time I was tempted to doubt Father Higgins' prudence. I had grown up with one or two boys who had entered mission seminaries, and I felt I was not at all vain in considering myself superior to them both physically and mentally. I realize now, of course, that Father Higgins was right, that God's good pleasure is always best, and I suspect that my youthful vanity was somewhat greater than anyone knew, especially I.

Buttrick came around the corner of the corridor and fixed his hand firmly on my arm.

"Come with me," he whispered.

The rules were strict in those days and, I believe, they still are rather severe. We weren't supposed to speak to our fellow students or visit their rooms after night prayers. However, there was an urgent quality in Buttrick's voice and manner which caused me to exercise *epikeia,* that convenient moral principle of self-dispensation from man-made rules when circumstances clearly indicate that such would be the will of the lawgiver were he on the scene. In other words, I followed Buttrick to a room which I immediately saw to be Willoughby's.

"Steady," said Buttrick. "You'll have to brace yourself for this."

He softly opened the door and I looked in. At first I could see nothing; the room light in those days came from a single desk lamp which barely illuminated the desk. Then I saw Willoughby lying flat on his back on the bed, covered by a patch-quilt coverlet which was evidently the work of a devoted mother. His eyes were open wide — very wide — and staring with that madly ecstatic stare at the naked ceiling.

"Is he dead or alive?" I asked flatly.

"He's alive all right — breathing deeply. But he won't come out of it. I've shaken him, punched him, even slapped his face. Here — I'll give his hair a pull."

Buttrick yanked at the dark locks and came to me with several hairs in his hand. There was not the slightest sign

6

of pain or surprise on Willoughby's face. It was as though he were a fakir.

Then for the first time I realized that there was a pungent scent of incense in the room. I walked around the bed and saw an incense thurible resting on the floor, with little wisps of smoke, barely discernible in the semidarkness, rising beside the bed. By now my eyes had grown accustomed to the gloom; I knew that the vestments were black as soon as I saw them resting on the room's only chair.

"Black vestments, incense, a trance — what can it mean, Buttrick?"

He paused for a moment and then said quietly, very quietly, "I don't like to think what it means."

A feeling of horror rippled across my chest. I looked around the room wildly. I knew then that something was missing, something which was part of the standard equipment of every room in the seminary.

"The crucifix!" I all but shouted. "Where's the crucifix?"

The question was purely rhetorical. The crucifix no longer hung in its usual place on the wall. It was not to be seen.

I felt sure then that this was not a little Halloween joke cooked up by Willoughby and Buttrick to shake my well-known complacency. Until this point, despite the feeling of horror, I had not entirely ruled out such a possibility. In a closed environment, even normal people sometimes fall prey to a distorted sense of values. But the absence of the crucifix excluded any practical joke. No normal seminarian, however devoted to humorous antics, would remove his crucifix from the wall.

Now it was I who spoke quietly. "I think we had better call in Father Higgins."

Buttrick's eyelids flickered and I thought his cheeks were redder than they had been a few seconds before.

"I wouldn't do that, George."

"Why not?"

"It's obvious, isn't it?" He smiled slightly.

I thought for a moment. "I suppose you're right. No sense creating too much of a stir. Maybe we can rouse Jack out of this thing, and then go on from there."

I did not want to think ahead too far, but I knew that it might come to a point where we would have to force Willoughby to resign from the seminary.

"George," my companion said, "you go and get Joe Broome, the student infirmarian. Maybe he can help, but you've got to persuade him not to talk. I'm going to call up a doctor friend of mine for a little advice."

It took me more than ten minutes to find Joe Broome. By that time the fire bells were ringing brazenly throughout the building.

Joe never heard what I had to tell him, because I turned on my heel and ran for Willoughby's room, which was in the east wing.

I was too late. The corridor was in flames and the fire was spreading quickly. I was beaten back by a barrier of smoke and fire, although I tried my best to break through. My cassock was charred in places, and my hands and face were scorched.

We were all standing on the lawn when the firemen came. I pointed out the window of Willoughby's room and they threw up a ladder and ran the hose in through the window.

I do not care to recall or to record the scene. Hours later the fire was finally put out. A charred skeleton was all that remained of the body of my friend. I dreaded to think of what had happened to his soul.

All of us, faculty and students, stood around in various degrees of undress watching the east wing burn to a ruin. The rector, Monsignor Heath, was remarkably calm as he tried to check attendance on the lawn. Of course, he could not be certain of the number who had escaped because we were somewhat scattered.

8

We were shocked when the firemen found another body, later identified as Buttrick, in the telephone booth.

It was almost dawn when, at the Rector's command, we left the grotesque scene.

"The seminary will be closed until further notice," he announced. "When I am assured that it is safe to resume operation, I shall notify you by mail."

His voice grew husky. "You will also be informed of the time and place of the funerals." He looked old and ill, I thought. It would have been strange if he had looked otherwise, standing there by the base of the statue of Our Lady of Perpetual Help, making such an announcement as this.

My own room and all my belongings, few as they were, were destroyed. I had to borrow clothes from the more fortunate, and in these I made the long bus trip home.

After the funerals, there was a two-week lapse before the seminary reopened. During this time, my mind fought to find the right path to follow. Day after day, I weighed the arguments for action and inaction. Should I tell the authorities what I knew? And if I did tell, what good would come from it? Of course I had little doubt that Willoughby's incense had caused the fire. He was dead. What could be gained by relating the horrid story of his last hours, a story so fantastic that it might bring more suspicion upon me than upon him?

I decided to put it out of my mind. However, a mere decision could not quell either my memory or my imagination. Again and again I found myself lost in the thought of that half-lit room with its prone but staring body and its pungent odor of incense.

Strangely I was not too surprised when the Rector called me at my home in the middle of the second week and asked me to meet him and "some other gentlemen" at the seminary the following day.

I was not wrong in suspecting that an investigation of

the cause of the fire was under way. The two gentlemen, I discovered, were investigators from the insurance underwriter.

The Rector introduced me to Mr. Brannigan, a stout, jovial man of middle age and Mr. Hobbs, a bald man with a white mustache and a nervously twitching left eye.

"Take the chair by the window, Mr. Roland," the Rector said quietly.

I looked and saw that the bright sunlight was pouring in the window on the proffered chair. It seemed evident that I was to be the victim of some sort of third degree. But the Rector was smiling reassuringly.

"I might explain, Mr. Roland," he said, "that you were seen entering the room of Mr. Willoughby on the night of the fire. No doubt you have a good explanation for this rather unusual circumstance. You see, these gentlemen feel that the fire originated in the general area of Mr. Willoughby's room. They thought you might be able to throw some light on the matter."

With these words, he glanced at the dazzling light coming through the window, and smiled again — reassuringly.

I tried to force an answering smile, but my effort was weak. In a way I felt both frightened and annoyed. I was fearful of telling the extraordinary tale and I was resentful of being put under pressure in the presence of two lay investigators. For a moment I thought of walking out, but I knew at once that this course of action was both imprudent and unnecessarily heroic. I decided to tell the facts in as limited a way as possible, omitting anything which might be damaging to Willoughby's good name.

"Mr. Roland," said Hobbs, "I think you should know that we found in Mr. Willoughby's room an overturned censer."

Rather dramatically, I thought, he lifted a scorched object from behind the Rector's desk.

I was unspeakably tense; I am sure that I jumped slightly in my sunlit chair.

"Do you recognize this, Mr. Roland?" Hobbs almost whispered. I was almost disappointed that he did not sound more like a district attorney.

At this moment, a feeling of calm took hold of me.

"If you'll excuse me, Monsignor," I said, turning to the Rector, "I think this procedure is unnecessarily dramatic. I can tell very simply what happened that evening and then if the gentlemen wish to ask me any questions, they surely may do so."

The Rector nodded.

"I was informed that my friend, Mr. Willoughby, was indisposed, and so I went to his room to see if I could be of any help. Having seen him, I thought it best to seek out the infirmarian. While I was doing this, the fire broke out and from that point on I have no more information to offer. It is true that I did see a lighted censer on the floor near my friend's bed and I must admit that I do not know why such an object was in his room."

"Can you think of any possible reason why a seminarian would have a censer in his room?" This was the first and last question the stout man asked during "the interview."

My mind was strangely sharp. "In answer to such a general question, I can say that there might be several possibilities. He might have been practicing the use of the censer."

"But I understand he was three years from ordination to the priesthood," the white-mustached gentleman snapped.

"I was asked for possibilities, not probabilities, Mr. Hobbs. In any case, younger seminarians use the censer in some ceremonies. There might have been other reasons too."

"Such as?"

"Perhaps he had discovered that burning incense cleared his head. Remember, he wasn't feeling well."

"Just what was wrong with him, Mr. Roland? Wait, we'll come back to that. What other possibility do you suggest for the presence of the censer?"

"Perhaps he was cleaning it. I don't know."

"Why would he be cleaning it? Was he the sacristan?"

"No. I'm afraid I can't say why he should take it upon himself to clean the censer. I suppose we all do unexpected things like that at times."

I began to feel rattled again. Hobbs's eye had stopped twitching and he seemed to sense that I knew more than I was telling. A complacent little smile was seeking control of his face.

As I look back on the whole incident I am inclined to feel that the Rector handled the affair badly. He should have called me in privately, asked me for what information I had, and then decided what course of action to follow. A seminarian should not have been subjected to this type of interrogation. However, I suppose the old man was perplexed and under a strain; his judgment must have been affected.

Hobbs spoke again: "Could you tell us a little more precisely what was ailing Mr. Willoughby when you went in to see him?"

I knew that hesitation might be disastrous here; I answered quickly, perhaps too quickly.

"He was very pale, lying on the bed. He didn't look well at all."

"What did he say to you?"

Here was a real test of my vocation. I had never been so strongly tempted to tell a lie. It would have been so easy to say, "He asked me to go for the infirmarian, because he felt sick to his stomach" or some such falsehood as that. But I was a man of principle, a seminarian; if anything, I tended to be overscrupulous in moral matters. I could remain silent about irrelevancies but I could not, would not tell a direct lie.

"He said nothing."

"Nothing? How did you know he was sick?"

"I could tell at a glance. No words were necessary. Besides, Mr. Buttrick had already informed me of the fact."

There was a pause. The Rector stared tensely at the floor. The smile disappeared from Hobbs's mouth. Even Mr. Brannigan seemed less jovial.

"Mr. Buttrick?"

"Mr. Buttrick met me in the hall and asked me to come to Willoughby's room. Surely the person who saw me enter the room must have told you about Mr. Buttrick."

"Yes, yes, of course." Hobbs's voice was smooth, conciliatory. "I hope you're not taking offense at these questions, Mr. Roland. We're not accusing you of anything; we're just trying to get at the facts."

I knew that a defensive tone, despite my resolution to the contrary, had colored my voice. But they were prying too much. What mattered all these details? It was clear that somehow the censer had fallen over and the fire had caught on. Surely it couldn't make any difference whether or not Willoughby was guilty of deliberate arson. He was dead, horribly dead — which in itself was proof of his innocence. Or was it?

Were they hoping to sue his estate? I knew he had been wealthy in his own right.

"Why did Mr. Buttrick think it necessary to call you to the room? Couldn't he himself have gone for the infirmarian?"

"Naturally. I imagine he was on his way to do just that when he met me. Then it probably occurred to him that I might be of some help to Mr. Willoughby."

"Help? In what way?"

"I don't know. In any case, I looked in the room and then went for the infirmarian."

"What did Mr. Buttrick do?"

"I believe he went to telephone the doctor."

"What doctor? Was it the regular seminary doctor?"

"He did not give me the name of the doctor he intended to call."

The Rector looked up. "Wasn't that a little irregular, Mr.

Roland? According to the rules of the seminary, Rule 67, I believe, only the infirmarian is authorized to call the doctor."

"I'm afraid I can't answer for Mr. Buttrick's conduct, Monsignor."

"Perhaps he thought the matter too urgent to wait for the infirmarian's arrival?"

"Perhaps, Monsignor."

The Rector nodded. "A case of *epikeia?*"

"No doubt."

Hobbs looked in amazement at the old priest, who seemed pleased to have eliminated a violation of rules from the matter under investigation.

Hobbs began to walk back and forth in front of the Rector's old mahogany desk while he continued his questions.

"We are all still a little puzzled about Mr. Willoughby's illness. Surely there must have been more alarming symptoms than you have described, to warrant such haste in calling a physician. Think very hard, Mr. Roland, and try to remember anything that might give us a clue as to what was really ailing him?"

"Is that so terribly important?"

The white mustache quivered ever so slightly; Hobbs halted abruptly.

"Yes, Mr. Roland, it is very important."

"I don't know what to add, Mr. Hobbs. He was lying on the bed; he was very pale and strange looking — obviously sick. I had been told by Mr. Buttrick that he was ill; I looked in the room and the fact was evident; I hastened to get the infirmarian. Mr. Buttrick took it upon himself to call a doctor; I cannot answer for Mr. Buttrick's course of action."

"What did he say to you?"

"He said 'I'm going to call a medical friend of mine for a little advice.'"

"Didn't that seem to you a little odd?"

"I didn't give it much thought. I was in a hurry to find the infirmarian."

Hobbs had resumed his pacing.

"Were Mr. Willoughby's eyes open or closed?"

I knew I was in danger again.

"They were open."

"Open? Well, then, did you notice anything peculiar about his eyes?"

"Peculiar? In what way?" But I knew my stalling tactics would not avail.

"Were they bloodshot?"

"I couldn't tell; I didn't study them that closely."

"Were they fixed on any object?"

"He seemed to be staring at the ceiling."

I stood up and walked to the window. Outside the Japanese ginkgo tree flamed in the sunlight. There was a flight of black sparrows against the sky. I thought: I'll have to do something to stop this line of questioning or there will be a horrible scandal. This affair will become known all through the insurance company; there will be talk, lots of it; there will be leaks; soon it will be whispered all over the diocese that a devil-worshiping seminarian set fire to the seminary while in a diabolical trance.

I turned to the Rector, who seemed in a sort of trance himself.

"Monsignor," I said, "may I ask for a little recess? I'd like to get a drink of water, clear my head, review some of these points that have been raised. Perhaps I'll have more light to give if I have a little more time to think."

The Rector looked at Hobbs, who gave no sign of either approval or disapproval. Brannigan smiled and nodded his head in consent.

The Rector stood up. "Very well, Mr. Roland; your request seems reasonable enough. Suppose we expect you back in this room in fifteen minutes?"

15

I tried to walk casually from the room, but my eagerness must have been evident. As I closed the door, I heard laughing, pleasant not mean, but nevertheless disturbing to my youthful dignity.

I walked to the water cooler at the end of the hall and drank a long swallow, then stepped out into the open cloister. The cloister consisted of a covered quadrangular ambulatory with a green yard in the center. A statue of Mary, Cause of Our Joy, stood in the middle of the greensward, and I said a brief prayer for guidance. As my feet clacked on the cement walk, I wondered if I would ever really attain the priesthood. I had nearly four years more before ordination; it seemed an endless time. Besides, I felt an uneasiness, a foreboding that some personal evil for me would come out of the strange circumstances of the fire and its aftermath — evil breeding evil. To my mind there was a diabolical cast over the whole affair. Some way or other, I felt, I would be made to suffer. Perhaps I would even be dismissed from the seminary. Why or how I could not imagine, but there was a very real sense of threat accompanying me in my walk around and around the cloister that bright November day. I did not even think of what I would say to further questions; I could only trust, trust that I would be able to answer truthfully without revealing the deadly scandal of Willoughby's diabolism.

I looked up suddenly and saw figures passing the glass doorway. Instinctively I hurried to the door and looked down the hall. Hobbs and Brannigan were on their way out the side door to the seminary grounds. I could see the flicker of matches as they lighted their cigarettes. I looked at my watch. There were nine minutes until deadline. I ran to the Rector's room and knocked softly.

"Mr. Roland? You're back early."

"Monsignor, I want to tell you something before those men return."

He hesitated a moment, weighing the ethics of the situation. Did this proposal violate some obscure rule of proper conduct?

"I don't know, Mr. Roland. I wouldn't like these gentlemen to feel that we had secrets, were withholding information. Everything is supposed to be above board. I deliberately avoided interviewing you in advance for that very reason."

"I'll leave it to you, Monsignor; I'll leave it to your judgment if they should know what I'm about to tell you. It could mean a great scandal for the seminary."

His eyes reflected his decision. "Sit down. What is it you wanted to tell me?"

I looked at my watch. There were seven minutes left. Hurriedly I told him the whole truth, the strange ecstasy in chapel, the rigid trance in the room, the absence of the crucifix, the presence of the black Mass vestments.

As I spoke his face grew even more pale than usual and his lips actually quivered.

When I had finished, he sat silent and still for what seemed like a full minute.

"I believe," he said slowly, "that in view of what you have said, I ought to tell you that Mr. Willoughby had a history of epilepsy. He was admitted to the seminary with the understanding that he had been cured. But it is clear from what you describe, that he had a seizure on the night of the fire."

"But, Monsignor, what about the missing crucifix, the Mass vestments, the lighted censer?"

The old man smiled gravely. "They do not disturb me. We have had other seminarians who have tried practicing the Mass ceremonies on their own, so to speak, years before ordination. Why, only three years ago I caught a first philosopher with a folding altar in his room. Very much against regulations, of course. Rule 23, I believe."

"The missing crucifix?"

"It might have been broken by accident. Or he might have knocked it accidentally behind the desk when he had

17

the seizure. Nothing to worry about. Of course he must have knocked the censer over in a later spasm. A very costly spasm indeed."

There was a knock. He looked calmly toward the door. "They know about the epilepsy. That's what they were trying to pin down. I think you can tell them everything they want to know. They will be fair; they are not trying to convict Mr. Willoughby of a crime."

I felt deeply ashamed while I answered the remaining questions.

I was hardly surprised when Hobbs and Brannigan concluded that the fire was caused by the censer's being overturned during an epileptic spasm on the part of John Willoughby deceased.

But even today, although I may be uncharitable, I still wonder about the probability of the Rector's explanation of the lighted censer, the black Mass vestments, and especially the missing crucifix.

CHAPTER II

My FIRST assignment in the priesthood was to what is known as a country parish. Actually the church, St. Victor's, was located in a sizable river town, old, ugly, but possessing a certain rugged charm by reason of the solid, determined people who inhabited it. Like many other up-river villages it had seen better days. There had once been two or three big furniture factories there, but the advent of cheap, jerry-built goods had led to their abandonment. There was still a chemical factory on the outskirts of town, but apart from this, small local businesses offered the only opportunities for employment.

Harwell seemed to be a town without a future. The homes were mostly old clapboard houses, cheaply built and ugly. Except for two apartment houses, I dare say there weren't more than a dozen "new" houses in the whole parish, and these could hardly be called attractive. I was amazed, in going in and out of homes in the course of my duties, to observe the musty Victorian-style furniture and to see that so few homes had central heating. Kerosene stoves in the principal rooms seemed to be the common lot.

The population of Harwell had for twenty years remained

almost static. The nearest big city was too far away for easy commuting although some ambitious souls did make the trip every day. Of course there were no big throughways at that time. Consequently most of the natives seemed content to live and die in their almost private world.

The people, although hardly zealous for new ideas, had a splendid tradition of loyalty to their parish church — a fact which made working among them a pleasant experience in many ways. However, they always referred to me as "the new priest." I am sure that Father Planter, the first assistant, who had been stationed there for eight years, was happy to surrender this title to me.

The nature of the town with its limited possibilities had rendered most of the youth extremely unambitious. It was not unusual for even a bright lad who had gained honors in the local high school to settle down to life employment as a gas-station attendant or a grocery clerk. One of my first surprises was to discover that the president of the Holy Name Society, a well-spoken, intelligent man of about forty, was employed as a cashier in a "beanery" on Main Street. He could easily have passed for a high executive in an important big-city corporation.

The old pastor, Father Mulvey, then nearly ninety and confined to his room, was a legend in the area. Often older parishioners would stop me on the street and tell me with relish of Father Mulvey's earlier exploits.

"I was glad to hear you raise your voice in the sermon on Sunday," a bent old lady informed me one day on the street. "Ah, Father Mulvey, there was a preacher, poor man! He would really make the pews jump and the parishioners as well. It's been told me as the absolute truth when he raised his voice he could be heard all the way across the river at Redville, and this with the doors and windows of the church closed! I hear he can barely whisper now — isn't it a pity!"

The gnarled oldster who delivered the evening paper

would often speak of Father Mulvey's activities "before the factories closed down."

"Every payday, regular as clockwork," he told me, "the Pastor would make the rounds of the factories to collect the 'parish dues' as he called them. He didn't care to wait until Sunday morning, what with Saturday night coming in between. And if the Pastor had heard a bad report or if he hadn't seen a man at the rail in a good time, there could well be a bawling out right on the spot. And what a bawling out! I've seen men without an ounce of shame in them blush scarlet when the Pastor uncorked on them. He really kept us in line, he did. A grand priest in every way."

Other parishioners, although in general agreement with the old delivery man, did not hesitate to note certain flaws in the Pastor's temperament, in what might be called the middle period of his life.

"You'd never know him now as the same man," one informant told me. "He's got very benign and easygoing in his late years — mellow, I guess you'd say. But years ago curates never lasted very long around here. We were always having new priests. Why, I understand on more than one occasion new assistants would arrive by one train and leave by the next, it was that bad. Quite a temper the Pastor had then, and he was very strict in his rules for the young priests. But he's mellowed now I guess you'd say, being confined to his room and all that."

Certainly he was mellow when Father Planter brought me into his room on the day of my arrival. He was attired in a faded bathrobe and well-worn slippers, rocking back and forth, back and forth in an ancient wooden chair. He peered up at me from beneath his bushy white eyebrows with a glance that was keen and penetrating.

"Yer welcome," he croaked, as my legs trembled. "This is yer home now. Remember that. Anything you need, within reason, anything you want to do, within reason, ask Father

Planter and he'll give you the O.K. I'm afraid I can't be of much help to yer. I used to do more when I was younger."

I was awkward then. I suppose most newly ordained priests are awkward, not only with the laity but with older priests. After all, I had no idea of how priests talked to one another, and of course the proper attitude toward a pastor was a complete mystery — except that I presumed they should be treated as was the rector of the seminary by the students.

Stiffly I said, "Thank you, Father. I hope that you will find my work in this portion of our Blessed Lord's vineyard satisfactory."

The old man chuckled and made a gesture to Father Planter. "Take him out, Father. It'll all rub off in a few weeks."

He continued to chuckle as we departed. At the time I ascribed his odd reaction to approaching senility. Naturally, I am better informed at present.

Those first days and months in the priesthood are precious in my memory. Everything was new and beautiful. I had an eagerness for routine work which I have never been able to recapture. My dealings with the parishioners were marked by a holy solicitude which leaves me staggered when I think of it. It may have left them staggered too, because I know that many puzzled and perhaps amused glances were directed at me in the parlor, and looking over my earliest manuscripts, I am forced to admit that my sermons were somewhat remote from reality.

Inwardly I enjoyed a satisfying peace of soul marred only occasionally by doubts as to the correctness of my advice in the confessional or the wisdom of my counsel in the rectory. Although I never formulated it to myself explicitly, I felt that my arrival had ushered in a new era in the religious history of Harwell. Not that the previous priests hadn't done good work, but there seemed to be so many things that hadn't been done.

I organized a study club and a high school sodality and revitalized the Altar Boys' Society. My predecessor had been barely able to provide one server for Mass. I appointed two and sometimes three and insisted on regular attendance with threats of dire punishments such as detention after school and the writing of lengthy compositions.

I held committee meetings for one project after another and zealously harangued the handful of loyal meeting-goers on their responsibility to stir more of their absent brethren to greater activity in "the cause."

I look back with admiration at Father Planter's restraint. He gave me my lead tolerantly, all the more so, I suppose, because he was a very tired man himself and stood in extraordinary awe of my amazing energy. Needless to say, many of my projects flopped badly in due time, but some of them were permanently successful, although not as dynamic as I had hoped.

I need not recount all of my early activities, but there is one haphazard incident which had more effect on my influence in the community than any of my carefully planned endeavors. I don't know whether a moral should be drawn from the occurrence, but certainly it proved to me that God's planning is of a much superior caliber to mine.

I was snoring contentedly one night when the phone rang loudly in the hall closet. At that time it was considered wasteful to install a phone in every room. Numbly I threw off my blankets and stumbled into the hall. I remember stubbing my toe on the door jamb of the closet. In any case I put an end to the terrifying clangor of the bell by lifting up the receiver.

"St. Victor's," I said in a dull, unenthusiastic voice.

"Chief Barnes, Police Department, Father. Couple of men injured. Chemical factory. Pretty bad."

"What's that?" It was all a little too fast for my sleepy brain.

23

"I'll be over as soon as I pick up the Mayor," was his only explanation.

I stubbed my toe again walking into the bathroom, and then I stood stupidly blinking into the mirror. I have never been at my best when awakened from sleep.

Nevertheless, I was waiting at the door when the police car pulled quietly up to the curb. I was vaguely disappointed that the siren was silent.

Fingering the container of sacred oils in my pocket, I hurried professionally toward the car. But then a disturbing question entered my awakening brain: Should I make the car wait while I obtained Viaticum from the church tabernacle or would this cause too much of a delay?

"Hello, Mr. Mayor. Chief, can the injured men receive Holy Communion?"

He shrugged impatiently. "I don't know, Father. S'not my line."

I hesitated. If I did not bring Viaticum with me, I might have to make another trip — which would be very inconvenient at four in the morning. On the other hand, if I brought the Sacred Hosts, the men might not be able to receive, or worse still, the delay in going to the church, lighting the candles, opening the tabernacle, etc., might mean the difference between my being on time or being too late to help the injured men.

Such questions used to bother me a lot at that time. It was just inexperience, I suppose, with a light touch of scrupulosity. I was a little too frightened of not being the perfect priest.

As it happened, I made the Mayor and the Chief wait while I placed two small white Hosts in my shiny, new pyx, which had been used only five or six times.

At last the long black car rolled away, the Chief driving, the Mayor and I in the back.

The Mayor began to question me as to my liking for

the town, the parish, the pastor. Nothing was said about the accident, except that there had been some kind of chemical explosion.

The Mayor, although a Catholic, evidently did not know that a priest carrying the Blessed Sacrament is not supposed to engage in casual conversation. I was too timid to say this directly to so august a personage, but instead gave monosyllabic replies, hoping to discourage further talk. He must have thought me very rude. However, my plan succeeded and there was silence in the car.

Murmuring silent prayers to Christ in the Blessed Sacrament, I watched the dark rows of houses pass us in the night. They possessed a dignity, almost a mystery, which was entirely lacking by light of day. Here and there the shadow of a large tree fell across the street. It was like riding through a monstrous graveyard, and yet I felt a certain strange peace mingled with a sense of importance. I was the parish priest doing his duty even while the town slept its unknowing sleep. I cannot capture the feeling exactly in words, but I have experienced it several times in my priestly life. Perhaps it has no real significance.

It couldn't have taken us more than ten minutes to arrive at the factory. There were bright floodlights in the yard. A few policemen and others were standing about. The ambulance from the Weston Hospital (ten miles away) had not yet arrived. In the distance I heard the siren of the town fire engine.

The Chief pointed to an entrance at the side. "Right in there, Father. The doctor is with them, I think."

No one accompanied me into the factory, although I did not think of this at the time. The doctor, whom I met on his way out, jerked his thumb at the hallway behind him.

"Back there. Better hurry, they've got to be moved. They're in bad shape."

I pulled the oils out of my pocket and rushed forward.

Two men were lying flat on their backs on the floor. There were blankets wrapped around them.

As I bent over the first I almost gagged to see his charred face. He had been horribly burned but had not yet lost consciousness. He whispered his confession, I gave absolution, and hastened to anoint him. Only his face was exposed and I dreaded to think what the rest of him looked like. Deciding on the short, quick form of administering Extreme Unction, I dipped my thumb in the Holy Oil and anointed his forehead as I said the sacramental words. To my horror, which fortunately I controlled, the flesh of his brow flaked away at my touch. Then I gave the Last Blessing; it was clear that he could not retain Holy Communion.

I turned to the next man whose eyes stared at me wildly. He was evidently in a coma, but I shouted acts of sorrow into his ear as I had been taught to do in the seminary, and his eyelids flickered slightly. I administered what sacraments I could, spoke words of comfort, and, nauseous, hurried out of the building. An ambulance swung through the gate as I stepped into the yard. Somewhere near me a flash bulb popped. Hoses had been pushed through the windows in the center of the factory, and men in fire hats were calling hoarsely. Dazed, I stepped into the police car and was driven back to the rectory by a young policeman. This time the Mayor and the Chief did not accompany me.

After I had returned the Blessed Sacrament to the tabernacle, I climbed the two flights of stairs to my room and lay down on the bed in my clothes. I still felt weak and sick, as though I had not yet awakened from a disgusting nightmare. And yet, in a sense, I felt closer to reality than ever before. It was as though I had for the first time lifted a corner of the veil which had hidden "real life" from me for years.

Of course I had read and heard of tragedies all my life. The newspapers had made sure that no one was ignorant of life's darker side. But all these things had seemed academic. The seminary tragedy had impressed me, naturally, but I had been more of a spectator than a participant. Tonight I had played an important role, the most important role. I had been closer to the men than anyone but the doctor. I had spoken to them, consoled them spiritually, been beside them in a positive, active way at the most critical moment of their lives. My priesthood, then, was not simply an abstract, textbook affair; it was a real, living presence and operation, on the scene, a thing of power, strength, beauty, grace — call it what you would — and the burned men were not characters in a sort of mental play, but men in real, horrible pain on the brink of a terrible death — and they were glad and happy to see me — me, at such a time.

I realize that I am not making myself too clear, but the experience which I describe defies accurate or complete definition. It gives one a sudden new insight into life's structure, a momentary awareness of values and realities never before perceived. And then it is gone — leaving behind who knows what greater degree of maturity and understanding than existed before. I can only say that, from that moment, I was never again quite as boyish and immature as I had been the day previous.

Actually, I am not so much concerned here with the tragedy as with its aftereffects upon my own life. The two men, I later learned, died in the ambulance on the way to the hospital.

Since the following day was my weekly holiday, I took the train to the city and spent a quiet time with my mother. I took a long nap in the afternoon and, with the resiliency of youth, I had almost forgotten about the accident when I arrived at the rectory late that evening.

I admit I was surprised to see lights in both the Pastor's and Father Planter's rooms; usually my confreres retired, country-style, irritatingly early.

Father Planter intercepted me on the staircase. His expression was grave.

"May I see you for a moment, Father?"

I wondered what I had done wrong, resolving at the same time to be meek at all costs although firm in upholding inflexible principles.

"Sit down, Father."

This atmosphere of formality was unusual, odd.

I rebelled slightly. "What's it all about, Jim? Why are you and the Pastor up so late? Why this nineteenth-century approach to a simple conversation? What has happened?"

He looked at me sternly for a moment.

"Don't you like it here, Father? Would you like to get out and go to a big city parish? Is that your ambition?"

My meekness was taxed slightly but I assumed an air of injured nobility.

"Of course I like it here. I have no ambition of the type you mention. What's it all about?"

He stood up, walked to his desk, and picked up a newspaper. He stared at it for a moment, and then shook his head in apparent despair.

"Father, you have committed the unpardonable offense of becoming a hero."

"What?"

"You heard me. Look at the county paper and see for yourself."

At this he was forced to break down. Laughing, he punched me (rather hard) in the chest.

"Nice going, George."

I studied my picture on the front page. It was not a good likeness, in my opinion. I looked groggy and unshaven, and seemed startled by the flash bulb. Over the picture there was a three column headline: "Heroic Priest Risks Life to Console Dying."

Sickening, I read the article completely. It seemed that

there had been danger of further explosions when I entered the factory. The injured men could not be moved out until the proper stretcher facilities had arrived. Disregarding all danger, I had rushed to the side of the dying men to administer the Last Rites of the Church.

So the article went. There was no effort to characterize the doctor as a hero. Presumably no one had thought to take a picture of him emerging from the factory.

Ashamed, I stared at the floor and told Father Planter the truth.

"I didn't have the slightest notion that there was any danger. Everyone seemed perfectly calm. I don't understand it. Not at all."

Father Planter sat back in his green leather chair and put his feet upon the ottoman.

"Well, you might as well face it: you're a hero and there's nothing you can do about it. But I must say, you've created an awful mess. People have been calling up all day, wanting to congratulate you. A few wanted advice in marital matters. The county radio wants you to go on tomorrow. The paper wants a human-interest interview. It's sad."

I thought for a moment.

"Why is it sad? What's sad about a priest performing an act of heroism? Why, this will be great for the Church in this county."

"Maybe you're right, but I doubt it. The Pastor agrees with you, however. He's all excited, insisted on staying up till you returned. You'd better go down before he falls asleep in the chair."

My enthusiasm for my own heroism had cooled in this brief moment. Instead a scruple began to take shape in my conscience. I voiced it to Father Planter.

"What am I to do? I'm in fact not a hero. I am receiving unmerited praise. What do you think? Must I issue a denial to the paper?"

Father Planter choked on his Phillie.

"That's a very sound idea," he said at last.

"You think so?"

"Of course not," he snorted. "Imagine what an absurd situation would develop. You deny you're a hero and either they believe you, in which case you and all of us are made ridiculous — or they don't believe you, and you're even more of a hero for trying to be so modest. Any way you look at it, you would do better to remain silent. I don't see that you have any obligation to issue a denial."

"You don't?"

"Even if you had known about the danger, you'd still have gone into the factory, wouldn't you?"

"I don't know. I suppose . . ."

"Of course, you'd have gone in. Any priest would. That's positive."

"Yes, I guess so." I preferred not to think of the hypothesis. I have never had a high estimate of my own courage.

"The Pastor's waiting."

Father Mulvey was solemn as he grasped my hand. His voice trembled even more than usual.

"You've brought honor on the parish. Thank you."

I was silent for a moment. Why should I disillusion this old man? Without comment, I expressed my appreciation and mounted the stairs to my room.

I had a strange dream that night. First I was pursued down a long corridor by a shapeless monster. At last I spied a door at the end of the hall. I escaped just in time through the door — alas! only to fall into a tank of flaming chemical. The flames were consuming me; I was smothering with the smoke when suddenly the entire scene was changed and I found myself in the Bishop's office (where I had never been) while the elderly prelate pinned a large medal on my cassock. Placing his right hand on my left shoulder, he said sonorously, "Because of your achievement for God and country, I am appointing you vicar-general of the diocese with the title of Right Reverend Monsignor."

I know that I was filled with shame. I wanted the position and the honor, and in a confused way I knew that this was very wrong of me. I resolved to preserve integrity regardless of personal sacrifice.

"Your Excellency," I said firmly, "I confess that I am a fraud."

There was a pause, and the Bishop began to roar with harsh laughter. Then, suddenly, he was transformed into a formless monster. . . . At this point I awoke.

It seemed a strange coincidence to find a letter from the Bishop at my place at breakfast that morning. He did not appoint me vicar-general, a position which usually went to a priest at least fifty years old, nor did he state that the Holy See was prepared to honor me with the purple, but he did extend his compliments on my "courageous action" so much in keeping with "the traditions of the priesthood, especially of the priesthood of this diocese."

Father Planter studied the letter as I began to empty my plate of the six pancakes which Becky, the maid, had served to me as a sort of reward, I presume, for heroism in the line of duty.

The older curate folded the letter carefully and replaced it in the envelope.

"You'll want to keep this," he said. "They don't come too often. But there'll be another soon."

I suspected what he meant but I pretended innocence. "What do you mean?"

"Simply that you're lost to us now. You've come to the Bishop's attention in a favorable way. Some day soon there'll be some sort of special opening for a young priest. He'll naturally think of you, and suddenly your little visit to Harwell will be at an end."

I admit I smirked a bit at this. I was — and am — as vain

31

as the next person. But my exultation was brief, for as I looked around at the bright little dining room with its gay chintz curtains and its cabinets of sparkling china, I knew that I was extremely happy at St. Victor's and that, despite my youthful restlessness, I had no real desire to depart. As I thought about it, I became slightly alarmed; all my projects, now just getting under way, would collapse at my transfer. I shuddered at the tragedy this would imply for the parish. . . .

The incident created quite a flurry in the town for some time. People coming to the rectory merely for Mass cards would ask for me by name, whether or not I was "on duty." Marriage arrangements were allotted to me. The lines, already long, lengthened still more outside my confessional. I found the altar boys more eager to serve than ever before, and my words were listened to with a greater awe both in church and at society meetings. A Catholic Action cell which I had just launchd caught on at once, giving promise of unexpected results in leavening the town with Catholic ideals and influences. In a word, this bizarre occurrence in which I merely performed the routine duties of a priest without any thought of possible danger or any effort at heroic conduct seemed to mean all the difference between mediocre and great success in my priestly activity.

Naturally a banquet was held in my honor. A committee of leading laymen, including non-Catholics, had sprung up almost spontaneously and plans were quickly laid for a gigantic supper at the Trollers' Inn, the only restaurant in town worthy of such an historic event. Tickets were sold readily, I understand, at well above the cost of the dinner, with the result that I was to be presented with a new Ford car (they were considerably cheaper then). I must say that my conscience was in a turmoil of scrupulosity at all this, and I tormented my spiritual director with questions as to my obligation to restitution. Although he reassured me that what was happening was beyond my control, I lost many an hour's sleep over the trap which had locked around me. Integrity, utter sincerity — these had always been the foundation blocks (so I imagined) of my spiritual edifice, such as it was.

By an odd coincidence the Mayor and the Chief of Police called for me on the night of the testimonial banquet. When I saw the sleek car pull up to the curb, I thought, for a terrible moment that my guilty lack of heroism had been unveiled. Certainly, I reasoned, the Mayor and the Chief should realize the absurdity of the claims which had been made in the paper. Certainly they should remember that they hadn't said a word to me about possible danger in the factory.

But, to my amazement, they were extravagant in their congratulations, the Mayor stating somewhat fatuously that this was "the best thing that ever happened to this town." The Chief shook my hand solemnly and said,

"I'm glad you didn't tell me about the danger, Father; if I'd known about it, I don't think I'd have let you go in."

I swallowed and looked away. I could not say anything in reply to such a remark, but I couldn't help thinking that the Chief was a very stupid man. I wondered if he had forgotten that it was he who first notified me of the need for a priest at the factory. How then could I have had more knowledge about the explosion than he?

The absurdity tickled me and I began to laugh.

"A little nervous, eh Father?" the Chief asked. "I know how you feel. I'm the same way about banquets. I guess you'd rather rush into an exploding factory any time."

The Mayor enjoyed this hugely. In fact, they were a great team, the Chief and the Mayor.

I sat between them and rode sorrowfully to the Trollers' Inn. Father Planter had gone ahead in his own car and the Pastor, although willing and anxious to attend, had been forbidden once again by his doctor to leave his room.

33

A reception committee, already well lubricated with *spiritus frumenti*, as my nose attested, met me at the entrance with much saluting, bowing, and handshaking. I had barely time to pull down my jacket in the back and square my shoulders before we marched into the festooned restaurant to the tune of "For He's a Jolly Good Fellow," sung lustily by all the paying guests.

At last we were seated, and the food and drinks were set before us. I remember regretting at the time that I had sworn off liquor for five years. In this situation drink was the only solution.

I shall not enumerate minutely the painful details of this occasion. Suffice it to say that a semiedible dinner of fried chicken was served, that garrulous and absurd speeches were delivered by countless town dignitaries, that I was presented with the keys to the new Ford, and that I made an inept and sheepish response to all that had been done for me. Even now, as I write, I blush at the thought of that evening. When I returned to the rectory after the banquet, I needed all my native restraint to prevent myself from phoning the Bishop to request a transfer so that I could begin my priestly life with a clean slate, though also with a new Ford car.

The ironical climax of my adventure in Harwell came just four months after the testimonial dinner.

I was "on duty" in the rectory when the phone rang at nine o'clock in the evening.

"Father?"

"Yes."

"This is the Chief."

"What can I do for you, Chief?"

"Father, I'd like to send the car for you. We need you out here at Skillen and Third right away."

I thought his voice sounded odd. "Is it a sick call?"

He paused. "Not exactly, but it might be before the night's over. I'll explain to you when you get out here."

"Now listen, Chief . . ."

"Father, you'll have to trust me. I can't explain it very well over the phone. You'll have to be here to understand the situation. I'm sending the car."

He hung up and I stared in puzzlement at the receiver in my hand. I wondered if the Chief had been drinking.

However, the black car, driven this time by a sergeant and minus the Mayor, crept up to the curb a few minutes later.

I slipped the oils in my pocket and walked into the night.

The sergeant was uncommunicative and I did not feel in the mood to press him for information. However the mystery was dissolved in a few minutes when we arrived at the apartment house on the corner of Skillen and Third.

There were several police cars lined against the curb, and about half a dozen officers were standing in close against the building. The Chief beckoned me into the lobby.

"Is someone hurt, Chief?"

He led me into a corner.

"That's what I want to avoid, Father. That's why I called you."

I looked around the glossy lobby, empty except for one policeman stationed at the elevator.

"Isn't it about time you told me what it's all about, Chief?"

He put his hand on my shoulder and stared at me from beneath his beetle brows.

"I wouldn't ask just anyone to do this, but I know the stuff you're made of. Once a hero, always a hero."

"Get to the point, please."

"Well, here it is. We've got Vicious Val Dowd cornered up in Apartment 5-E. There's one door, no fire escape. He's armed and he's desperate. If we try to rush the door, it's almost certain that one, possibly several of our men will be killed. He's got a peephole in the door and he can shoot right through it. He's already yelled out that he'll shoot anybody who even tries to go near the door."

I felt absolutely cold and numb inside.

"Where do I fit in, Chief?"

"Father, I think if you would walk up to that door and talk to him through the peephole, and perhaps get him to let you into the apartment — well, I think you could persuade him to surrender without any bloodshed. Many of these fellows will listen to a priest, and only to a priest. You could point out to him that he can't escape anyway, and that it would be much better if he came out without shooting."

I was incredulous. I found myself getting angry at the Chief's presumption.

"What do you take me for, a sitting duck, Chief? Why don't you use megaphones from the street to shout up your messages?"

"We've already tried that. He took a couple of shots at one of our men."

"Has he got a telephone?"

"The wire's been cut."

I sat down on a lobby bench for a moment's thought.

This would be a grand exit for a "heroic young priest" — shot full of holes by a vicious killer. The trapped man was not called "Vicious Val" for nothing. Or, if the Chief's plan worked, I could keep the new Ford with an easier conscience. But the idea was ridiculous because it was unnecessary. The Chief was in too much of a hurry; in a few days "Vicious Val" would have to come out or starve to death. Or they could cut through the ceiling or wall or let someone down from the roof in a bulletproof basket — as I thought it over, there were any number of ways in which, if the Chief were patient, he could capture Vicious Val without my walking into a flock of bullets.

I stood up and explained my point of view to the Chief. He seemed surprised, hurt, let down.

Finally he said, "But, Father, after the way you acted at

36

the explosion, I thought a heroic young priest like you . . ."

"Sorry, Chief," I said, "I am not now and never was a heroic young priest. But I'm not a fool, either."

Once more, I walked out into the night.

I do not think that this incident had anything to do with the fact that I was transferred to St. Bede's in the city ten days later.

CHAPTER **III**

ALTHOUGH I was born and brought up in the city, I found the transfer to a city parish very trying — at least for a while. This is, I gather, the usual reaction of a priest in these circumstances. In the country (as any place outside a central city is called) a priest — even a very young priest — is a person of considerable importance in and to the community. He is a public figure known to all, Catholics and non-Catholics alike. When he walks down the street, he is greeted in a friendly manner on all sides. He is known and usually respected by the mayor, the superintendent of schools, the newspaper editor, the president of the bank, and the grocery clerk. His presence is more or less expected at civic functions and any word of either praise or criticism of the community on his part is listened to with great attention and often brings tangible results of some kind.

All this I had discovered, enjoyed, and taken for granted in my brief stay at Harwell. My first experiences at St. Bede's were a cold contrast to what I had known. I discovered that my presence in the crowded, tenement community made little impact on anyone — including the pastor, Monsignor Haggerty, and his three veteran assistants.

Hardly anyone nodded as I walked along the avenue that

first day. A few children did say "Good afternoon, Father," but this was done in a rather perfunctory, impersonal way, clearly the result of coaching by the nuns in parochial school. On the whole no one seemed too surprised or interested that a new priest had appeared in their midst, and I could not help feeling a little heartache at the apparent coldness. And as time went on, I was to discover that although the city priest may be an important part of his community, he is rarely a dominant figure in it. Of course, this is in the nature of things. A major city is too big and too sprawling, and so-called "communities" are too ill-defined to allow for a notable influence on the part of any but the most outstanding individuals. Moreover, the interests of city dwellers are so scattered in so many areas and the parishioners are subject to so many diversions that the local priest can hardly expect to be in the center of their thoughts for any considerable length of time.

In spite of these observations, I must confess that greater experience has taught me that the difference between the country and the city is perhaps not as great as I believed it to be at the time of my first change. It is amazing how small-townish parochial life can become, even in a large metropolitan area. However, it took me a while to learn this.

Even in the rectory the atmosphere seemed different. The older assistants were cordial but, it appeared, rather impersonal. A few perfunctory questions were asked, I was given a few directions, and then I was left alone, presumably to fend for myself. Actually several weeks passed before I came to spend more than a few minutes in conversation with any of my fellow priests. When I say "few minutes," I exclude those rare mealtimes when all of us were assembled around the same table. The Pastor was not a man to encourage talkativeness on the part of a young priest less than a year ordained.

In mentioning these facts, I do not mean to portray this

as a typical situation in a city rectory and, in fact, my first impressions in this case, as I have hinted, were actually false. They were simply impressions which were heightened by contrast with what I had known and which were made all the sharper by my limited experience in dealing with priests and in facing new situations in the priesthood. In time, I was to have a very happy rectory relationship both with the Pastor and my fellow assistants.

However, I cannot forbear to repeat my first interview with Monsignor Haggerty, if only for its singularity.

He greeted me rather pontifically, without rising from his lounge chair.

"You may come in, young man. I should like to instruct you on several points about your work here."

He had a handsome visage with straight hair, still black, and pale gray eyes, almost belligerent in their cold stare. Two or three chins hung over his collar — the principal detriments to what otherwise would have been a striking appearance.

I remember that he held a large cigar in his hand and clouds of pungent smoke gave the huge, half-lighted room an almost oriental air. Dimly I could see long, high bookcases filled with beautifully bound volumes. The desk and tables were of carved mahogany and the easy chairs were covered with cardinal-red plush. The Turkish carpet sank under my plebeian feet.

A sense of my immaturity and inferiority came over me as I stood before this regal figure. He did not ask me to sit down.

"I would not deceive a young Father," he said in his deep, well-modulated voice. "The work here is very difficult. If you are to do your duty well — and I don't tolerate any other type of conduct — a great deal of self-sacrifice will be demanded of you."

He stretched his legs and pulled on his cigar.

"Of course," he continued, "the absence of this spirit to which I allude — the spirit of self-sacrifice — is at the root of most of the difficulties of our generation. It presages the decay of our civilization. It would be sad indeed if the excessive desire for ease and comfort and the like were to infect the clergy. 'If the salt lose its savor . . .' You know the quotation."

I shifted on the Turkish carpet and nodded. I decided that I was going to sit down even without an invitation. From my position on a straight-back chair I could see into the enormous bedroom. The red silk spread on the outsize four-poster seemed rumpled. I judged that the Monsignor had already had his nap.

"Make yourself comfortable." He waved an approving hand at my bold expedient of seating myself. "And now to business. I suppose you realize that this is a very busy parish?"

"Oh yes, Monsignor. But that won't be any problem to me. We were very busy in Harwell."

"Ho! A-ho! Ho!" This is the best reproduction I can give of the laugh which greeted my solemn affirmation. For several seconds he coughed and sputtered.

"Excuse me. A-ho-ho-ho! That's rich! Very busy in Harwell! Priceless!"

My cheeks began to redden, but I resolved not to engage in a fight at my first interview with my new boss.

Now, of course, I understand his reaction. He had never been stationed in the country, having gone from the seminary right into a large urban parish where he had remained until his appointment as pastor of St. Bede's. He had the all-too-common notion that "country" priests had nothing to do but offer Mass and hoe their gardens. He would have been amazed at the amount of Church activity in a small town like Harwell. I began to explain but he brushed my comments aside.

41

"Excuse my outburst, but that's the best thing I've heard in a long time. Well, young Father Roland — it's 'Roland' not 'Boland'? — yes, young Father Roland, if you worked hard and were very busy in Harwell, you're really going to be active in St. Bede's. We've always had only three assistants here but I asked the Chancery for a fourth because we have so much work. That's how you happen to be here. I told the Chancellor we needed an extra priest — I specifically asked for a young priest, and I must say you fit that specification perfectly — to wash the sacred linens, to take charge of the altar boys, and to carry on the youth work of the parish."

I swallowed. It was interesting to note the order in which he listed my special duties. I wondered if he considered "doing the linens" my most significant function.

He looked impatiently toward the bedroom.

"To put the matter briefly and somewhat bluntly, Father, we have something of a juvenile delinquency problem in this area. You'll find out as you go along. Most of the people are of good, honest Irish stock and they and their children live decent lives. But there are some real slum areas where the people live in wretched hovels and their morals match their homes — some of them anyway. Are you of Irish stock, Father?"

I have always resented questions of this type. Such inquiries strike me as crude and beside the point, almost malicious in their implications either of inferiority or smug superiority.

"Partly," I replied as abruptly as politeness allowed.

"Then you know," he said, his eyes narrowing wisely, "that no one is worse than a bad Irishman. The dirty Irish are really dirty, and so are their children. Unfortunately we have quite a few of this type in the parish."

His eyes veered once more toward the adjoining room.

"Do what you can for them, will you? The boys, I mean.

42

They haven't had enough attention up to now. Every week we get a call from the police, or some mother comes in with a sad story about her son. Do what you can. I'll back you up, give you whatever financial help you need — within reason."

He stood up and ostentatiously suppressed a yawn. I wondered if he was going to invite me to share in the bounty of the mahogany cigar box.

Instead, he said, "If you'll excuse me, I think I'll take a brief nap. I didn't sleep too well last night."

My eyes squinted in the direction of the rumpled spread.

"I'll see you, Monsignor," I said and slammed the door a little harder than necessary. I am almost sure I heard the creaking of bed springs as I marched belligerently down the long hall toward my narrow sitting room.

In those days I rarely took a nap — I have since acquired greater wisdom, or perhaps merely age — and hence I sat at my desk and stared moodily for a half hour or so at a bleak pad of paper. Finally I picked up a pencil and began to write:

"1. The pastor here is hard to figure out. He seems to envision himself as some sort of bishop.

"2. The other priests are older and don't seem too interested in me.

"3. I have to take charge of the youth work — which is O.K. — but I don't know what's been done or what should be done or anything about it. The pastor said, 'They haven't had enough attention up to now,' so I guess I'll be starting almost from zero.

"4. However, I organized a number of things in Harwell, and I guess I can organize youth activities here. This is a good chance to show some real zeal."

I put the pencil down and stared for a moment at the old wooden crucifix on my desk.

Suddenly I felt very tired. I yawned and stretched. I decided to take a nap, after all.

43

My efforts at organizing youth work proved to be a partial success. My chief weaknesses were inexperience and a desire to be liked by the boys with whom I was dealing. This last tendency can be almost fatal. Boys, as someone once said, are peculiar people. If you treat them rather roughly yet justly, and once in a while give them a smile and a word of encouragement, they'll probably worship you — if you happen to be a priest. But if you coddle them, and crack too many jokes, and go out of your way too often to be nice to them, they will become either familiar or insolent and probably end by despising you. This is not a new observation but it is unfortunately one learned only by experience. One has to find out by trial and error what is the proper attitude proportioned to one's own personality and the boy's temperament. Of course, I've seen some men who were so reserved with youngsters, so eager not to appear overeager that they made no contact at all and left the kids unimpressed and uninfluenced. On the other hand, although much has been written on the evil of flattering our superiors, little comment has been made on the danger of flattering those under us. It is a prime hazard of youth work.

I succeeded in improving the attendance of the altar boys by means of the co-operation of the Sisters in school and by promising frequent rewards for services rendered, namely, trips to the ball game, movies, etc. I hired an excellent athletic director for the parish, a young law student who had made a national reputation on the football field while in college. This fact alone served as a great magnet for boys of all ages. He built up a good athletic program and soon our teams began to win most of their games — basketball, of course, being the chief parochial sport.

I started a Newman Club in the public high school, although this turned out to be something of a disappointment in terms of numbers enrolling. I was more successful with the grammar school released-time classes. With the help of pudgy Father Osborn's Sodality, we increased the attendance 25 per cent.

All this was good. In fact I was quite proud of myself for having accomplished so much in the space of a few months. But actually I realized that I had hardly touched the gangs, the real centers of what had grown to be a serious delinquency problem in the parish. These boys, with a few exceptions, just didn't "come around," unless occasionally to use the gym on a rainy night.

Father Osborn gave me a tip.

"You won't draw them without dances," he declared one evening from the well of his huge leather chair.

He scratched the wart on his nose and added, "Have a basketball game every Friday night followed by a dance or, maybe better, roller skating, and you'll draw even the delinquents. In fact that may be the problem: you will draw too many of them and there will be trouble, plenty trouble."

I was enthusiastic at once.

"Skating," I said, "skating is absolutely the thing. A lot of these boys would be ashamed to dance, but skating they can do. You've solved my problem."

He wiped his bald head with a gray handkerchief and looked at me innocently.

"There are one or two angles you'd do well to consider before you launch a big program."

"Such as?"

"Such as what you're going to do with these lads once you bring them to the church hall. How are you going to approach them? What are you going to say to them? How are you going to influence them? Basketball and roller skating aren't going to eliminate delinquency by themselves."

"Thanks. I'll work it out. The first step is to get in striking distance of them."

I already had a plan worked out. Once I made the initial contacts, I would gradually win the confidence of as many

45

of these boys as possible, making a particular effort to meet and to see frequently the leaders. I might even drop into their clubhouses. I might offer to obtain for them better facilities or invite them to make greater use of the church's equipment. Once they accepted me as someone genuinely interested in them, the chance to eliminate the delinquency incidence of these groups was great. I began to visualize myself as the Father Flanagan of the slums.

Success was slow. I finally got the skating parties under way and was pleased to find them extremely popular — in fact, too popular. It came to a point where we were turning boys and girls away from the box office because of lack of space. The floor was always jammed and angry complaints were voiced again and again about pushing and bumping.

It seems that every remedy creates new diseases. My skating parties, designed to reduce the pressure of the "youth problem" in St. Bede's, led to new difficulties which demanded new solutions. Girls began to appear in abbreviated costumes, which made me fear for the preservation of local modesty. Bottles of liquor (this was in Prohibition days) were smuggled into the hall in duffle bags, and once in a while a boy would pass out in the lavatory. Sometimes there were fist fights on the floor and I heard more than one spate of foul language. Mothers at times called me at the rectory to complain about the late home-coming of their precious daughters who had gone on the town after the skates had ceased clicking. There was breakage in the hall — chairs, windows, fixtures; and breakage, of course, is a very sensitive point with pastors.

However, Monsignor Haggerty, remote in his paneled sitting room, was philosophical about these difficulties, and generous with the church funds.

"The people in St. Bede's," he ruminated one day as I was giving my report, "are the salt of the earth but it is rough salt. In other words they are generally uncouth, and naturally their children take after them. Go ahead with the skating, but try to have better supervision even if you have to hire a couple of ex-policemen for the evening — in other words, bouncers."

Ex-policemen were the last persons I wanted if I was to gain the confidence of delinquent gangs but I did manage to hire a couple of sturdy ex-firemen, and this together with a big slash in the number of tickets sold, helped considerably to improve the situation. But there still remained the problem of how I was going to pick out delinquents from the surging mass and then approach them successfully in the general hubbub of a typical Friday night.

The first part was relatively simple. Nearly every teen-age boy wore some sort of jacket with the name of his gang or club printed on the back. Most of these "gangs" were merely athletic groups without any connotation of evil-doing. But I learned from one of the altar boys that "The Panthers" and "The Champs" were "really mean" and that, moreover, there were frequent "rumbles" between the two groups. A Champ, he said, had been clubbed to death in a vacant lot within the previous year. Naturally the Panthers were suspected.

On the night I chose for my preliminary approach, I stood at the side of the rink and watched the skaters roll by. After ten minutes of observation I could see only two jackets with the "Champ" trademark. There was one "Panther" jacket. Certainly my skating enterprise had not drawn the delinquents in large numbers.

My plans had been carefully laid. Calmly I fastened my skates and took a tentative whirl around the floor. The skaters, flushed yet serious in their pleasure, ignored me for the most part although a few made the shy impertinences which are presumably characteristic of teen-agers when they see their local priest on skates. My retorts were gay but I too had serious business in hand: I was going to knock down a delinquent boy. I was resolved to meet the lone Panther and to meet him unequivocally.

Gradually I approached him from the rear. He was a good skater, graceful, tall, and slim. From my vantage point he seemed almost delicate, hardly the brutish type one would suspect as a murderous gang member. It would be too bad if I injured him seriously. However, I decided to take the necessary risk; to make a forceful and unmistakable impression at the beginning was absolutely necessary. This could not be done in this case by any of the usual methods. There seemed to me a certain delightful irony in my meeting violence with violence.

I hurried forward, pumping hard. I drew almost parallel to the black-haired boy, and then with a final effort, pressed so close to him that he was knocked off his feet and sent sprawling across the floor.

With modesty, I must confess that it was perfectly done. The other skaters skillfully avoided the prone gang boy, some bending down to help him to his feet.

I quickly wheeled over toward the gathering crowd. I could hear the young Panther's obscene curses as I approached.

He shut his mouth when he saw me but glared violently from dark eyes. For a second a sense of uneasiness pricked me. Would this mean that retribution would fall on my head in the form of a street attack some evening by a pack of Panthers? Not if I carried out my plans carefully.

I held out my hand.

"Sorry, kid. I was skating too fast. Sometimes I play a little rough."

Slowly he held out his hand and I thought I saw a flicker of admiration in his eyes. I noticed that there was a scratch on his cheek and that it was bleeding.

I turned away and grunted over my shoulder.

"Follow me."

I gave no explanation for this peremptory invitation, but I heard him coming after me.

I led him to a basin in the locker room and pulled down the first-aid kit.

"You've got a little scratch. I'll fix it. I shouldn't play so rough."

He snickered. "You're not so rough. Maybe a little clumsy. You wouldn't know what rough is."

I pulled out some cotton and unstopped the iodine bottle.

He put up his hand. "I don't need that stuff. What do you take me for? All this big deal for a little scratch. Am I a baby?"

"You tell me. See if you can stand this without yelling."

He snickered again and set his teeth as I cleaned the scratch and applied the iodine. His eyes watered but he showed no other sign of pain.

"Your eyes watered," I told him.

"So what? That's natural. You mean your eyes wouldn't water?"

As he pulled a filthy handkerchief out of his pocket, a five-dollar bill fell on the floor. I said nothing but eased over and put my foot on the money. He was wiping his eyes, oblivious of his loss.

I made him give me his name and address "because of the insurance company." He snickered at that.

"You think I'm going to sue you?"

"Who can tell?" I said.

He started to move away, toward the skating floor.

"Thanks for the iodine," he said. Then, "Next time try not to be so rough."

He enjoyed this sally. When he had gone I bent down and picked up the five-dollar bill. I smiled complacently as I put it in my pocket.

The following afternoon, my hand clutching the precious bill in my pocket, I walked briskly into the "Jungle." This was the name given by one of the more sensational tabloids to the area where lived Jerry Jabunski (my injured friend of the previous evening). Discreet inquiries brought me to the basement room where he and his fellow Panthers had their lair.

As might be expected, a group of them were playing cards — poker, I suppose. There were chips on the table. All four of the boys were smoking; I saw no liquor at the time.

Fortunately they did not reach for guns or knives when I appeared in the doorway, but a big red-faced youth said, "This is private, Mister. No admittance."

I saw Jabunski staring at me for a minute; then he looked at the bill in my hand.

"So you found it, Padre."

He stumbled over to me with his hand outstretched. For a moment I was distracted by the lewd photographs on the walls.

"Yes," I said, "you look as though you might need it." I glanced significantly at his small pile of chips.

He took the bill in his hand and turned to his comrades.

"This is the padre that runs the skating parties and knocked me over last night. Here he returns my fiver I lost. He's O.K."

The red monster snorted.

"None of them is O.K.," he said. "Anyway you got your fiver so come back home before the cards get cold. Drop in again, Padre, when you find some more fivers."

His tone was so insolent that I found it difficult not to punch his nose, rash as such an action might have been.

I said, "Thank you. I will drop in again, maybe with something better than money."

Jabunski snickered. "What's better?"

"Booze maybe," the redhead commented. "Or babes."

He was really mean.

50

"Wait and see," I said weakly and climbed into the sunlight once more.

I had made my contact. After that I had to develop it into something worthwhile, and this took time. I did visit the clubhouse again about a week later to offer the Panthers the use of our gym one evening a week. Jabunski said he would talk it over with the other members. The redhead was not present on this occasion. Jabunski told me that there were about forty boys in the gang. He did not bother to thank me for my offer.

The following week about ten of the Panthers, led by Jabunski, appeared at the gym to "work out" as they called it. The redhead was absent. However, I felt that I had accomplished a great deal in a short time. I reported in an optimistic tone to the secluded Monsignor Haggerty that my campaign to deliver St. Bede's parish from juvenile delinquency was, in its beginnings at least, a solid success.

His eyes looking wistfully toward the bedroom, he cautioned me, "Don't fall into the ever opening trap of over-confidence. Endings are the best test of beginnings — particularly where youth are concerned. They break your heart nearly every time. I would not have you scarred — not more than necessary, that is. And now, if you'll pardon me, I had very little sleep last night."

But I was not fearful of disappointment. From my point of view, there was nothing to lose, since the juvenile gang situation could hardly be worse. Anything I was able to do by way of bringing these boys under my influence was a great improvement over past conditions. I felt that in time I could accomplish much. It might take two or three years but eventually bad gangs would cease to exist in this area. I had no serious doubt about this. Working through Jabunski who, I discovered, was highly respected by the rest of the gang, I was confident that the majority of the Panthers could be brought in line. Of course there might be a few boys, like the red brute, whom I could not reach, but there would not be enough of them to form a gang.

I was shocked to learn one morning from Father Osborn that Jabunski had been stabbed to death the previous night in an alley not too far from the clubhouse of the Panthers.

"I got the call from the police," the bald priest told me. "He was dead on arrival. I gave him the Last Sacraments conditionally."

My head was still whirling with this harrowing information when I was called downstairs to the parlor to see what Sheila, the maid, accurately described as a "big redheaded woman."

As I stared into her bloodshot eyes, she explained to me that her son Joey was being held as Jabunski's murderer.

Then I recognized her face; she could only be the mother of the red-haired Panther.

"Why should they hold a Panther for the murder of a fellow Panther? It doesn't make sense," I said.

Her loud baritone voice cracked as she answered.

"That's what I said. But the cops said there was jealousy in the gang. They say Joey wanted to get rid of the Jabunski boy."

She pulled out an absurdly small handkerchief.

I felt like asking her why she hadn't taken proper care of her son in the first place, but such a remark seemed hardly in good taste at the moment. Instead I asked her how they had connected Joey with the crime.

"They found the knife in his closet. I swear I don't know how it got there, but then I'm not home much. Anyone could have put it there. Anyone. And some other boys in the gang have squealed and said that Joey was bragging he would get Jabunski sooner or later. But you know how kids talk. I know Joey's a rotten little bum, but he's not a murderer. I know that. I know it. He hasn't got the nerve; he's just like his father used to be."

Despite the tragic nature of her remarks, I was glad that she hadn't said, "My boy is a good boy." This I would have found hard to stomach.

"What do you want me to do?"

"Help him, Father. That's what priests are for, isn't it? Speak to the D.A., the judge, get him a first-class lawyer. Do something to help this innocent boy — bad as he is in many ways."

At this point the red-haired, red-faced woman howled miserably.

"I'll see what can be done," I mumbled, and quickly escaped to the calm safety of my sitting room.

Older heads advised me to keep hands off the affair. The boy deserved no special help. Let the law take its course. If I became involved, I would lose a lot of good will on the part of Jabunski's friends, and all my work would be ruined. There was no sense in going to the defense of a cheap, murdering punk who had stabbed another boy ten times in the back.

I went to see Joey in his cell in the county prison. He was bitter.

"It's you caused all the trouble," he snarled. "Everything was good until you butted in and Jabunski started getting Boy Scout ideas, taking down the dirty pictures and going to church to play basketball. And then when I want a rumble with the Champs, he and his pals won't play."

"So you announced you'd kill him. Right?"

"Big talk. Big talk. I don't kill nobody. Beat 'em up, maybe. No killing. Never."

"Who did it then?"

"The Champs. Who else? They knew we'd had a split. They figured they'd get two of us at once."

"Maybe I can help you."

He stared at me for a long time.

"You'll help me? You mean that?"

53

"Yes."

"Listen," he said, and he swallowed his pride in a big gulp, "if you get me out of this — completely, I mean — I'll even go to church for a workout. I mean it."

Because I felt reasonably certain that Joey had not killed Jabunski, I went to the police and to the district attorney and persuaded them to reopen the case for further investigation. They were reluctant but I convinced them. They thanked me about a week later when they broke down three Champs into confessing the crime. Joey's analysis had been correct.

After these events, my influence among the delinquents increased appreciably. I think I helped to reclaim several of them. Certainly, there were no killings or rumbles for many months.

However, my role as padre of the gangs came to an unexpected end just one year later. "The Jungle" was torn up by the roots. The city cleared the area for one of those enormous housing projects which were later to rise in every section of our town.

What happened to Joey? He began to come around to the church hall as he had promised. Before he and his family moved away to another town, he had started to live a fairly good Catholic life. I had lost track of him for a long time until a few years ago when I learned that he had died manfully at Anzio.

CHAPTER IV

I CANNOT, in reviewing my years at St. Bede's, escape the recollection of an occurrence that surpasses in poignancy anything else in my priestly experience.

The sequence of events began innocently enough.

After the altar boys' meeting in the church hall one Wednesday afternoon, Timothy Barrett, a brown-haired, dimpled lad of nine, waited to tell me that he had decided to become a priest.

I smiled and patted him on the head and told him that I was delighted.

"Keep praying for the grace you need," I said, "and keep on being a good altar boy and before you know it you'll be old enough to enter the prep seminary. I'll pray too that God will help you to stick to this fine idea."

I said a few other routine things. I was pleased but not overwhelmed. Altar boys of this age have a way of developing very temporary vocations. I did not know then that his was to be the most temporary in my experience.

Just before he left, he stared for an embarrassed moment at my shoes and then said, "I'm going to be a priest in St. Bede's, just like you. Do you think I could?"

"Sure, Timmy. Good boy. Run along now."

He walked from the hall with a new dignity that was both

touching and amusing. Grinning, I turned to see that the chairs were in order.

Naturally I was surprised when Mrs. Barrett called me during supper to say that Timmy had not yet arrived home.

I asked the usual questions: "Are you sure? Could he be staying at another boy's house? Had he ever run away from home?" She was negative in all her responses.

Two hours later a detective came to see me at the rectory.

He was a tall, slender young man, handsome, well dressed, and, I was to discover, very careful about his speech. He had removed his hat, thus destroying one of my illusions about detectives. He shook hands politely.

"I'm afraid I have unfortunate news for you about one of your altar boys. Timothy Barrett has disappeared."

"I know that," I said, sitting on the edge of the office desk. "His mother called me."

"When was that, Father?"

"A little after six."

He loosened his coat and pulled out a silver cigarette case. "Do you mind?"

I compromised a principle. "It's all right if the pastor doesn't catch you."

He consumed one fourth of the cigarette in one giant drag and then exhaled with slow contentment.

At last: "Father, did you see anyone standing around outside the church hall either before or after your altar-boy meeting today?"

"I didn't notice anyone in particular before the session. And I didn't leave the hall at the end for at least five minutes. I was trying to straighten up a bit. Monsignor Haggerty is fussy about neatness."

"I appreciate that, Father. Well, can you give me any information at all which might help us identify the kidnaper?"

"Kidnaper?" I almost shouted the question.

"Father, I don't think it's necessary or advisable to conceal the facts from you. We have definite evidence that the Barrett boy was kidnaped — probably just after he left your meeting this afternoon."

I could not believe this. His parents were not rich.

"How do you know?" I argued, without conviction. "He may just have run away. Boys often do things like that."

Sloane grimaced and dinged his cigarette in the empty wastepaper basket.

"I know, Father. I've had a little experience with these matters. But the boy was kidnaped or else there would hardly be a demand for ransom in the case."

"Mrs. Barrett mentioned no ransom demand to me."

"The call came just after you spoke to her. An anonymous voice on the telephone."

He flicked some ashes off his knee. I could hear the rectory phone ringing in the hallway.

"Incidentally, Father, what I've told you is confidential. We don't want to let the papers in on this until we've done as much checking as we can."

Molly, the fat housekeeper, waddled into the office.

"Phone call, Father Roland."

In a moment I had returned to the parlor.

"That was a reporter," I said. "Someone has informed the press."

"I suppose it's just as well. Who tipped them off?"

"You'd better ask them."

The horror of the situation began to work on me. I knew there was terrible danger — so often, it seemed, kidnaping victims were killed even if the ransom was paid. And yet this case was so inexplicable. To carry off a nine-year-old son of relatively poor parents — what could be gained?

"Why was he kidnaped?" I asked. "I don't imagine the parents have much."

"The voice on the phone asked for five thousand. He must have figured out that the family could raise that much from relatives, friends, the bank possibly."

"It was a man's voice?"

"Yes. We're trying to track it down. I've got to leave you, Father. If you think of anything, let me know."

He straightened his tie, picked up his homburg, smiled pleasantly, and left me.

I started to climb the stairs to my room when I heard the phone ringing again. Once more Molly called me.

The man's voice was thick as though he had been drinking, but his tone was courteous.

"Father Roland?"

"Yes."

"I'm sorry to bother you, Father, but perhaps you'd be willing to do me a favor."

"What kind of favor?"

"You've heard of the kidnaping of the Barrett boy?"

"I have."

"Let me introduce myself. I'm the kidnaper."

I looked wildly around for Molly but she was out of sight.

"Don't try to trace the call by holding me on, Father. I'm going to hang up in about one minute."

For a moment I was determined to try persuasion on this wretched human being. Perhaps, I thought, the appeal of a priest to his faith in God, to his human feelings, might prevail — somehow or other, I might be able to convince him that he should give up this immoral scheme, return the boy to his parents, repent of his crime. I began to speak:

"In the name of Almighty God, the All Merciful yet the All Just, I beg you . . ."

"I'm sorry, Father. The minute is passing quickly. If you want to hear what I have to say, you'd better listen."

I couldn't take chances.

"I'll listen. Go ahead."

58

"I want you to get five thousand dollars in ransom in five-dollar bills from the Barretts. Put the money in a small, plain suitcase. Tomorrow night at eleven-thirty drive out to the Old Mill Restaurant. You know where that is?"

"Yes, but it's been closed for several months."

"Right. At the back of the house there's a large box where the baker used to leave the bread early in the morning. Leave the bag in that box and go home. The boy will be released, safe and sound, the following morning. Is that clear?"

"It's clear."

"If there's any funny business, anyone planted in the house or spying around the grounds, I just want you to realize that I'll know about it, and the boy will never be seen alive again. Are you willing to promise that you'll carry this out just as I've said? I'm willing to take your word."

I saw an obvious opening.

"I'll have to ask the police. I can't vouch for this on my own authority."

"Naturally." The voice was thickly pleasant. "I'll call later for your final decision. I'll have to have your word or the whole arrangement is off."

The phone clicked.

Immediately I telephoned the police in the hope that the call might be traced in time. The effort, I learned later without surprise, was futile. The call had come from the bus depot where hundreds of people used the phones every hour. Meanwhile I tried to prepare myself emotionally for Detective Sloane's second visit, this time to advise me on my dealings with the kidnaper.

I remember feeling fatigued that evening. I lay down on my bed and stared at the ceiling, trying to regain my calm, to make a proper decision, and at the same time to put the whole matter out of my mind.

I lay there twitching nervously. At the time of which I

write, I had not yet lost youthful zeal, but nevertheless I had a natural loathing of "being involved." In projects which I myself initiated, no amount of trouble disturbed me; but to be drawn into a situation in which I was not in control but was being "used" by someone else or was being made to carry an unforeseen burden — such situations I avoided, and still avoid to an extent, although I have since learned, I believe, that the demands of charity may often be met only by "involvement."

My impulse on this occasion was to try to escape trouble. But I could not reason how I could do this and still be assured that everything possible was being done to save young Timmy Barrett, whose newborn "vocation" had been accompanied by such immediate tragedy.

On the way downstairs to see Walter Sloane, I accused myself of selfish thinking.

His first statement disconcerted me, although I had expected it.

"Father," he said, almost enthusiastically, "you hold the key to this case in your hands."

I chuckled mirthlessly. "So you think I ought to go through with it?"

He studied his manicured hands. "I've been instructed by the chief to advise you to do exactly what the criminal has directed. The Barretts feel that they can raise the money in time — friends, relatives, everyone is chipping in."

My palms were sweating. "You understand what I told you on the phone. I've got to give my word that I won't co-operate with the police in setting any trap. If I give my word, I stick to it, even with a kidnaper."

Detective Sloane stared happily at the picture of the Bishop on the wall.

"Father, we do not intend to ask you to co-operate with us in any way except to do exactly what the kidnaper wants. Is that fair?"

My conscience bothered me a little because I feared instinctively that he planned to spring his trap without telling me. But what could I do? What did I want to do? Certainly it was not my responsibility to question the police about their plans. The main point was that I was not knowingly involved in any trap.

"Fair enough."

When Sloane had left, it occurred to me that prudence would dictate a little chat with the Pastor. A second thought told me that prudence would dictate the opposite. Probably, like myself, he would be happy not to be involved. However, I felt the need to protect myself, not to mention the parish, from the ire of the Bishop in the event of unfavorable publicity. I climbed the heavily carpeted staircase and rapped on the massive door.

From the depths there came a hollow *"Entrez!"*

He was in his big chair, slumped well down, his legs stretched out on the ottoman. He looked thinner and paler than usual, and his normally cold eyes seemed softened by weariness. A book was on his legs. He lifted a languid hand and beckoned me in.

I explained to him the events.

His expression hardly changed during the recital, although I thought I detected a trembling of his lips. Toward the end, his eyes focused more sharply, and finally he asked,

"You have decided to act as go-between?"

"What can I do?"

"Yes or no?"

"Yes."

He nodded his head.

"I'm sorry the criminal did not speak to me; something else might have been devised. Now the only way you can save your good name as a priest is by capturing the kidnaper and finding the boy alive. Otherwise the Church will have received a serious blow."

I began to feel a little stress in my cerebral region. I had dealt with this man for two years now, but I still found him disconcerting.

"Even if the criminal isn't captured, Monsignor," I said slowly, evenly, "if the boy is recovered through my efforts, certainly that won't harm the Church."

"I disagree. In the first place, people have a contempt for go-betweens, and, second, once the boy has been returned, everyone will regret that the money was paid and that the criminal escaped. The man who made it easy for the kidnaper will not be held in high regard. They will say that the priest should have minded his own business and let the police take complete charge. The public is very fickle, Father, particularly where clergy are concerned; they're quick to find fault. Surely you've already experienced that. Anyone who assumes spiritual leadership has got to watch himself, I tell you. The mob as a mob is always tempted to crucify him because he's a threat to mob values; he has presumed to stand aside from the mob and be a person. Do you follow me? Am I rambling a little? I feel really tired tonight, but I must go out."

For the first time I noticed streaks of gray in his black hair; his eyes seemed watery.

But there was truth in what he said. However, those fine points were now beyond my control. I could not refuse an errand of mercy because "the mob" might later think ill of me.

"Would you have me refuse?" I asked. "Let the boy be killed perhaps?"

He shook his head. "It's gone too far now. The time to take a stand was when the criminal first called. I'm sorry I wasn't consulted."

I cleared my throat angrily. "Monsignor, he's going to call again. I'd be delighted to have you speak to him. I tried to reason with him but he threatened to hang up

62

This man knows exactly what he wants and he's not open to persuasion."

Monsignor Haggerty pushed himself up wearily from the chair. I almost extended a hand, so tired did he seem.

"No criticism intended, Father," he said. "It's too late anyway. He'll probably call about midnight and he's not going to change his plans at that late stage. You'll have to go through with it, but I feel sorry for you. I'm going over to see the Barretts. They'll need some consolation at a time like this."

I felt ashamed. I had not thought of consoling the Barretts. This tired Pastor could still teach me a few things about zeal.

I sat by the telephone in my room for most of the evening, trying to read Dom Chautard's *The Soul of the Apostolate*. I found it hard to concentrate even on the very simple language of the holy Cistercian. The phone rang constantly until eleven o'clock but the kidnaper was not among those who called. After eleven there was silence and I continued to read. It was clear from the book that my priesthood was markedly off spiritual center. There was not enough contemplation, enough attention to God's inner presence; there was too much concern with everyday trivia, too much energy expended in external works. Works, I read, should flow out from contemplation, not crowd it out of the soul. I looked up from the book and studied the crucifix. It was true that the problems and activities of this huge parish were beginning to drown out my consciousness of the super· natural. I would have to strive for greater recollection, greater detachment from the work I was involved in. Or else tepidity would win.

The bell rang me out of my reverie of self-accusation. I listened to the voice.

"Father Roland?"

"Speaking."

"Have you made up your mind? Are you in the picture?"

I paused; there was still a chance for persuasion. "Yes," I said, "but I'd like to say something to you about this whole proposition."

"Sorry, Father." His voice seemed less thick, rougher. "If you start preaching, I'm going to hang up. This is my party, not yours."

"I just thought . . ."

"Sorry. That's it." I could detect anger now. "Will you give me your word, Father, that there are no tricks or traps connected with your mission?"

"None, as far as I know."

"Father, you might just tell the police that there are more than one of us in this. If a cop is seen in the neighborhood of the Old Mill or if the one who picks up the money bag is spied on or arrested, the boy will be killed."

I lost control.

"You dirty monster! You scum!"

But my epithets were wasted. The phone had clicked. I was left fiercely clenching the earpiece, my chest filled with a savage frustration. As I thought of it, it seemed to me almost a sin to have anything to do with rewarding this mean, low, cowardly preyer on the poor and innocent. But I could not sit by and let the boy be murdered.

I called Detective Sloane and briefed him. I told him of the suspicion which was growing in my mind.

"How can we trust this man?" I asked, quite naïvely, I suppose. "I have an awful feeling that he'll grab the money and forget about returning the boy. It would be easier for them to kill Timmy; perhaps he's dead already. It seems a foolish thing to reward the kidnaper with five thousand dollars for a horrible crime."

Sloane was smoothly conciliatory, as though calming a hysterical woman.

"Let *us* worry about those angles; that's our job. The point is that most people, even hardened kidnapers, aren't going to murder a kid unless they figure they can't take the risk of returning him. In the second place, this rat is in the catbird seat. Remember that; he's in control. We can't take chances on this boy's life. We've got to do what the snatcher says, even though it's hard to take."

"I suppose." I felt embarrassed at having raised so obvious a question.

"I'll drop off the money bag for you tomorrow evening about seven. Agreed?"

"Agreed," I replied, and hung up the phone with a moist hand. Father Osborn appeared in the doorway of my room. He was dressed in black slacks and a red-checked shirt, his bald head glistening.

I recounted those facts which he did not already know.

"I think you need a Scotch," he said.

In a moment he returned with glasses, ice, soda, and a bottle of Red Hackle.

At that time I was not used to drinking highballs, or liquor of any kind for that matter, but this seemed to be a special occasion. In the two years I had been at St. Bede's it was the first time that Father Osborn had made this particular gesture of hospitality.

He poured me three ounces and added the same amount of soda. I gulped it greedily.

Not until a second round did I feel fully relaxed, and then I felt very relaxed indeed. Even now I can say that one drink is of little value to me. But two drinks are still my limit.

We discussed everything then except the kidnaping. Osborn told me to forget it until seven the next morning. I was willing, but even in spite of the Scotch, a slight tremor seized me at unexpected moments and I had to whip my thoughts away from the plight of poor Timmy in captivity — if he was still alive.

We talked favorably about Roosevelt — who still claimed our fealty at this time. We spoke unfavorably of the depression — which was still heavy upon us all. Hitler Germany disgusted us and we were not happy about Mussolini.

Halfway through the second Scotch I found myself denouncing in a heightened tone of voice lackadaisical pastors.

At this point the somewhat astounded face of Monsignor Haggerty appeared through the cigar smoke.

He stood for a moment studying the bottle of Red Hackle, the glass in my hand, the cigars, and my mouth which was half open.

He seemed about to condemn this orgy of self-indulgence, but then shook his head sadly and clucked his tongue.

In a moment he said, "I have just returned from the Barretts."

There was a tinge of righteousness in his voice.

"Naturally they are in a very bad state, but I am glad to say that they are finding great strength in the consolations of our holy religion."

His pulpit air was clearly coming on. I took a giant swig from my glass.

"I led them and the assembled group in the recitation of the holy Rosary and then I tried to present to them some motives both for trust and for resignation. It is a pleasure to report that they responded excellently and I left them in a much improved state. Perhaps you'd be interested in what I said to them."

Unconsciously I let out a great yawn — something I never do unless I have had two Scotches.

"Excuse me, Monsignor."

He looked at me with even sadder eyes than before.

"Well, perhaps tomorrow you'll be better disposed to learn what might be a useful pastoral lesson. I suggest, if I may, that you try to get a good night's sleep. Tomorrow will be a very important day."

I smiled and nodded him out of the room. Osborn, leaving a few minutes later, put a sympathetic hand on my shoulder.

"Don't worry," he said. "I don't think he marked you down as a drinker. He's slow to form judgments."

"That's good." I nodded happily. Actually I did not care. I just wanted to go to bed.

Thanks to the two drinks I slept rather well that night, but the following day was a trial. An uneasy sensation sat on the top of my stomach throughout the day. No matter how I tried to absorb myself in present work, the dread anticipation of my midnight task intruded. Unfortunately it was not a busy day. Parlor calls were few and the telephone bell was almost silent; the time dragged.

At seven Sloane came with the bag, a blue canvas one of the type used by boys to pack their gym equipment. I was surprised to find it so light.

He said. "A thousand fives don't come to much weight."

I nodded.

Sloane's right hand dipped into the pocket of his smart camel's hair coat and came up with a revolver.

"You'd better have this for the time being."

I could sense the blood leaving my face. Subconsciously I had been keeping the idea of personal danger in the background; now a police revolver accosted me.

"I don't really see the need for that," I said glibly.

"It won't hurt to carry it," he said. "You can't be sure what crazy thing a criminal will do."

"Whatever you say." With studied carelessness I put the gun in my cassock pocket; it weighed down one side drastically.

He held out his hand. "You're on your own, Father. We're not going to follow you or attempt any trackdown until the boy is released — if he is released. The main thing now is to get the boy back to his parents. We can't risk antagonizing the kidnaper now. You understand that. So you're completely on your own."

I tried to smile but my face was frozen.

"As I understand it," I said, "I'm just a messenger boy. I don't think we need to get too serious about my role in this affair."

His pale countenance showed no change, no flicker of agreement. He offered his hand and left the rectory.

At eleven-fifteen I climbed into my black Chevrolet and drove out of the city. The bag was beside me on the front seat; the revolver bulged the right side pocket of my overcoat.

I felt better when I had left the city behind and was driving along the highway. In ten minutes I would have dropped off the money and would be on my way home. I would be glad to be free once again.

A drive-in shopping center looked ghostly on the right. Only the dim lights of a bar and grill gave evidence of life. As I continued, there seemed to be large vague fields on either side of the road. I knew this route very well, I told myself. Suddenly, however, it seemed unfamiliar. I had not remembered the cabins on the left, or the dim gas station somewhat farther on. But I knew it was the correct road.

A car approached from the rear, gaining ground quickly. Detectives? I could see a mass of curly blonde hair as the vehicle sped past me. Hardly detectives. I chuckled at my thought. I was feeling better now. There could be worse jobs than that of messenger boy. There were no decisions to be made, hardly any responsibilities involved.

I reached the crossroads and took the right turn. The Old Mill restaurant, dark, desolate, was a couple of hundred yards down this road, to the right. I turned into the gravel driveway which led to the front porch. I saw no light of any kind; I shut off the motor and put the car key in my pocket. I stepped out of the car, then reached back to take the bag in my left hand. Instinctively now, I grasped the pocketed revolver in my right hand.

Slowly I walked around the side of the deserted restaurant toward the rear. There was just enough moonlight to make a flashlight unnecessary. I could see nothing suspicious, yet I was breathing heavily and I could smell my own sweat.

Arriving at the kitchen door I saw a large wooden box which, more than anything, seemed to resemble a small coffin. I lifted the lid and looked into the pale, dead face of Timmy. I straightened up with a wail of horror.

Immediately the bag was grabbed from my hand and a blackjack grazed my head. My assailant had tried to do two things at once and so the blackjack had missed. I turned to wrestle with him. If he wanted my car and my priestly clothes he would have to fight for them. A terrible loathing filled me as the horror of his crime penetrated my consciousness. At first, as we grappled, I thought I could not subdue him. I had never been much of an athlete and he seemed muscular enough, although I smelled liquor.

We rolled over and over. I could not pull out the gun.

His hands closed around my throat, tightening, strangling. Desperately I pushed him back far enough to bring my feet into play. Savagely I pounded my heels into his stomach. He fell back with a great cry and did not rise. I stood up and lifted Timmy, wonderful Timmy, out of the coffin made for bread.

I am not ashamed to say that I wept as I stood there in the moonlight, holding him in my arms while five-dollar bills scattered in the breeze and a heartless criminal writhed groaning in the grass.

The mendacious Sloane, who, as it turned out, had been hiding in the trunk of my car, appeared now with his handcuffs and his gun.

But I did not watch him as he secured his prisoner. My gaze was fixed on the bruised little face of the holy innocent, of the priest that might have been.

CHAPTER V

I HAD many odd experiences as an assistant at St. Bede's. I cannot attempt to summarize all that happened, even all the strange, unusual happenings. Besides, in this book I am trying to record just a few high points of interest, events which have interest value even apart from the fact that a priest was involved in them.

As I think back, one incident toward the end of my stay at St. Bede's, an uncomfortable incident for me, or for any priest, rises automatically into my consciousness. It concerned a marriage arrangement, with a very strange outcome.

Surely it is well known what the daily routine of a parish priest involves. I speak particularly of those days when he is "on house duty," as it is called. On other days he can usually use his time at his own discretion — for making parish calls, for appointments with converts perhaps, for preparing sermons, for organizing parish activities, for recreation. But when "on duty" — at least in a large city parish — the priest is expected to remain in the rectory all day and night, available at all times for consultation in the parlor and for answers over the telephone. Naturally he must also respond immediately to any emergency sick calls which come to him during this time. In most rectories the priest on duty sits in his room, studying, reading, following his hobby, writing letters until he is called to the parlor or to the telephone. The call having been suitably dealt with, he returns to his room to continue whatever he was doing until another call comes. In a small country parish, such a day on duty can be relatively quiet, with few interruptions, but in a good-sized city parish, a priest may well be running up and down stairs all day and sometimes even until fairly late in the evening.

This latter situation was the case at St. Bede's. It was difficult to concentrate on a book or sermon in your room because just as soon as you had relaxed in your easy chair and lighted your pipe the buzzer would ring to announce a caller. This would mean hustling downstairs again, with perhaps two or three more parishioners arriving to see you before you had taken care of the original visitor. An hour or more might pass before you returned to your book and then you might have to set it down again within five or ten minutes. Sometimes, you might decide to spend the day sitting in the parlor; but this would inevitably be a day of extraordinary quiet.

Usually, however, a day at St. Bede's would bring in most of the following items: a large number of persons to arrange Masses for the deceased; several individuals with religious articles to be blessed; a few people to "make a special confession"; three or four bums looking for a handout; a certain number of poor souls with difficult problems of conscience to be thrashed out with the priest; several women having difficulties either with (a) their husbands, (b) their daughters, (c) their sons, or (d) neighbors and relatives; a convert or someone poorly instructed in the faith seeking greater enlightenment; an alcoholic determined to take the pledge; an undertaker to arrange a funeral; some members of your parish social group to discuss plans for the next dance; a mother, on relief, seeking funds to tide her over until the

71

arrival of the next government check; a young man looking for a letter of recommendation for a job; a sick call; numerous requests for information both by telephone and in person; a couple or two seeking to dissolve their marriage; and a couple or two seeking to make arrangements to marry.

The next to last item is often the most involved and troublesome of all those mentioned. The last item can either be simple or complex, usually simple. One day, however, I became enmeshed in a marriage arrangement unparalleled, I think, in the long history of St. Bede's.

The couple interrupted me in the middle of "Amos and Andy," a fact which did not improve my disposition. However, I tried to be cordial, leading them into the small office which we used for marriage interviews.

The girl, Regina Wood, I already knew slightly from having seen her in the parish. She was attractive in a typical big American city way, well turned out with a pretty but not memorable face surmounted by auburn curls. Despite her seeming sophistication, it was clear after a few moments of conversation that she was blessed with that fresh simplicity and innocence of soul which seems, surprisingly, to flourish in the heart of even our most wicked cities. I liked her, her friendly yet respectful way of speaking, her sweetness, her openness.

The man was another matter. In the first place he was altogether too suave for my taste. Dressed like an international playboy, he had all the expected attributes of a seasoned man about town: the overcultured voice; the elaborate, almost obsequious manners; the thin, pale profile set off by a carefully combed mass of shiny black hair. I was particularly irritated by the way he held the girl's hand almost throughout the interview and the way he glanced at her with supposedly loving looks every time she spoke.

"We should like very much, Father, to be married on Saturday afternoon," he said. "Isn't that right, darling?"

72

She nodded, darting a somewhat shamed look in my direction. She knew that this was intolerably short notice.

I refrained from snapping. Rather I paused and made an act of resignation, resolving to be as cheerful and helpful as possible even though the "Amos and Andy" show was now irretrievably lost.

"It would have been well to come in sooner," I said pleasantly. "Banns have to be called three times, you know; that takes at least two weeks, and there are papers which are needed."

He replied quickly, with a regretful smile. "We are really so sorry, Father, to rush things like this. We had planned a later wedding — in a month or two, but my firm has just decided to send me to South America for a six-month study of local markets — I am associated with Patty-Cake Dresses you know — and the ship leaves Saturday evening. So you see the matter is beyond our control. We are forced to ask you to disturb somewhat the even tenor of your ways — or rather the Church's ways. Surely a dispensation of some sort is possible in a case like this."

There seemed to be an edge of contempt in his last remark, and even though he continued to pat the girl's hand, his eyes hardened.

I told myself that as a priest I must not dislike anyone, much less form prejudgments. I forced a smile.

"It is possible, under the circumstances, that the Chancery may grant a dispensation from banns. You will need testimonials, however, from a priest and a relative as to your freedom of state. I presume you're both Catholics; is that correct?"

"This is correct, Father," Regina Wood answered. The man nodded his head slowly, and I thought I saw his eyes flicker as he did so. I knew that I was going to be mighty sure of my facts before I married this man.

He produced two envelopes.

"I have already obtained my testimonials, one from a priest, one from a relative."

I read them slowly, first the sealed letter from the priest, a Father Gadger of St. Tiribius' Parish, which was located in a fashionable area of the city.

"Mr. Peter La Tour resides in this parish, although he has been previously unknown to us. He says that he attends Mass here regularly and that he has lived in the parish for more than two years. In checking our records I can find no previous marriage involving this man. I can simply state that I have no knowledge that he has been previously married or that he is bound by any impediments."

This could hardly be called a testimonial; it placed all the greater burden on me.

The other letter was from a cousin who stated that La Tour had never been married before and was free to contract marriage.

I looked at the girl, "Have you any papers?"

"I was baptized here and attended the parish school, and have lived here all my life. I don't imagine you need many papers in my case, Father."

"You're right," I said. "I'll check the baptismal records and you can bring your mother tonight or tomorrow to testify to freedom of state."

La Tour was eying me steadily, his face slightly flushed. I knew I faced a tussle.

"Have you your baptismal certificate, Mr. La Tour? It is a prerequisite in marriage arrangements."

"I am so sorry, Father. I was about to raise that point myself. Unfortunately the record has been lost although there is no question that I was properly baptized."

"Where were you baptized?"

"At St. Joan's Church."

I knew that it was located in a French-Canadian section of town.

"Why is there no record, Mr. La Tour?"

"I would like to know the answer to that myself. Evidently the priest who performed the baptism forgot to make the necessary entry in the records. Such things must happen from time to time. It's very unfortunate."

He shot his cuffs delicately and looked sweetly at Regina.

I laughed lightly. I was not going to be stiff and formal about this matter — just firm.

"That is unfortunate, Mr. La Tour. Of course, then, you must have other proof of baptism. Your parents are alive?"

"Unfortunately, no."

He bowed his head gravely and almost clicked his heels, despite the sitting position.

I stood up and walked to the window. The garbage cans were already at the curb in position to be picked up by the collector the following morning. The cats would have a good night.

"Are your godparents alive or anyone who was present at the baptism?"

"No, I'm afraid not. But is all this really necessary, Father? It's an odd thing to be asked to prove that I'm a Catholic after all these years of practicing my faith."

He glanced appealingly at Regina who sat stiff, staring straight ahead.

"Really," he said, "I had not expected an inquisition."

It was his first really nasty note, and he gave a humorless little laugh to cover his crudeness.

I was still by the window. The windows needed washing although the curtains were fresh. For a moment I was tempted to kick him out, but this was a mere flickering emotion. I could not arbitrarily deny people the right to get married provided they could establish their eligibility. Of course this was the question. Thinking of Loyola's phrase *"Suaviter in modo sed fortiter in re,"* I slid once more into the desk chair.

"I'm sure you're joking, Mr. La Tour. Marriage is a lifelong contract of a sacramental nature involving the most sacred and serious rights and obligations. For the protection of both parties, possible children, society, and the sacrament the Church wants to make as sure as reasonably possible that there is no defect in the marriage, no hidden impediment or barrier which would render the sacred contract invalid. Certainly a man of your intelligence understands that, Mr. La Tour."

His face softened although his eyes remained hard.

"Of course, Father. It's just the phrase you used, 'as sure as reasonably possible,' which might give room for some discussion. However, I think I have a solution. I have remembered some old family friends who were certainly present at my baptism. I'm sure they'll be happy to testify to that effect."

I felt that he was lying, but I could not guide my conduct by feeling.

"Good," I said. "Please bring a notarized statement signed by these friends, stating that they personally witnessed your baptism at St. Joan's Church. Let them also include a statement as to your freedom of state."

His face had a set smile now. The finger wave in his oily hair shone glamorously. The shine on his shoes was like that of patent leather. He pulled up his trousers a hitch at the knee to protect the crease. The air was redolent of bay rum.

"Making assurance doubly sure, eh what? Very well, Father." He started to rise. "Then we'll say Saturday at three for the ceremony?"

I became suave again. "There are just one or two other points before you leave, Mr. La Tour. I am required by Church law to make certain inquiries."

The beautifully arched eyebrows went up, possibly an inch. "Still more?"

76

Regina, who had been staring hypnotically at the floor, shifted uncomfortably.

I took down necessary information, names, addresses, parents, previous residences, and questioned them about possible impediments.

"Have you ever been married before?" I asked Regina.

"No, Father," she whispered, almost inaudibly.

"Have you ever been married before, Mr. La Tour?"

He laughed lightly, innocently. "I assure you, Father, that I am completely free of marriage entanglements."

"Yes or no?" I insisted.

"No."

My suspicions were heightened by his attempted evasion. His whole manner, appearance, everything suggested that he was the sort of man who'd been involved in at least one previous marriage. I renewed my resolution to check up as fully as possible.

Then I gave them the usual instruction on the sacredness of marriage and on its rights and duties. They both followed politely, raised no objections to anything I said. I gave special emphasis to the permanency of marriage and the immorality of contraception. His face showed smiling approval. Regina seemed to be in a sort of trance.

At last, "Have you any questions?"

They had no questions, except to inquire about the stole fee — which was ten dollars.

I stood up, glancing at my watch. Nearly an hour had elapsed.

"Of course," I said — suavely — "I must have all papers in my hands well in advance of the ceremony and naturally everything is contingent upon the Chancery's granting a dispensation from banns. I'll call them tomorrow."

Regina looked anxious for the first time. "Do you anticipate trouble, Father?"

I smiled. She was a delightful girl, pretty, sweet, naïve.

It was strange how she could have chosen this perfumed lounge lizard for a lifetime partner.

"I don't anticipate any trouble, Regina."

As they were about to leave, La Tour grasped my arm gently and said in a soft, almost confidential voice, "Regina and I would consider it an honor if you would personally perform the ceremony."

How suave could a man be? I suppressed a snarl.

"If I am able, I shall be happy to perform the marriage. It is the usual thing here for the priest who makes the arrangements to marry the couple."

"Thank you, Father."

My own suavity, I knew, had been dented somewhat, and I was not entirely at my ease when I returned to my room for what I hoped would be a quiet evening.

I released the thirty buttons of my cassock, removed my collar, and sank into my red plush easy chair. Tomorrow, I told myself, I would make several phone calls to check up on Mr. La Tour, the smoothest con man who had come my way in a long time. Tomorrow I would get busy. At the moment I felt like relaxing. I picked up *This Side of Paradise,* a book I had always wanted to read.

I saw a shadow and looked up at the bulking Father Burleigh. He was cassockless, his stomach protruding like a great half pumpkin. He sat down on my yellow leather chair next to a futuristic lamp on a modernistic table. The pumpkin dissolved into huge tirelike rolls. He looked around the room and nodded.

"You've got nice quarters now."

"You think so?"

"Yes. It looks like the lounge in a new movie theater."

"Is that a compliment?"

"That's up to you. I came in to talk about something — anything. I'm tired of myself — been alone all day."

"Well, I had a case tonight that could get me jittery."

I told him the facts, and he listened rather reluctantly. He never liked shop talk or sharing the problems. His advice was cryptic.

"Don't stick your neck out. Be very sure this is on the level before you go through with it. Otherwise it might very well bounce, and that would be bad all around."

My nervousness increased at this expression but I said, "Well, I'm not going to get all excited."

His jaw slumped gloomily into his chins. "You can't be too careful. I had an innocent-looking couple in here about five years ago. They were young and I wasn't too fussy about papers — just the minimum."

"What happened?"

"Bounced."

"Yes?"

"The boy — only twenty-two or three — had a wife and child in Wisconsin. You see my point? The Chancery really chewed me up for negligence. It wasn't pretty."

I pressed back into my huge easy chair. My brain pulse quickened. I resolved to work on my marriage case first thing in the morning.

I was restless in bed that night.

After breakfast the following day I managed to get a Father Buveau of St. Joan's on the telephone. I told him about La Tour's claim to baptism.

"Father," he said in compassionate French-Canadian tones, "I would be very hesitant to believe that there was a failure to record a baptism in this parish. We have always been very strict about it — it is a parish tradition to double-check. I would watch this gentleman La Tour very closely."

"Have you ever heard of that name around the parish?"

"Never, Father, and I've been stationed here for many, many years. It's strange that he never came in before about this question of baptismal records."

"Very strange." I was getting nowhere. "Would you do

me the favor of checking both your baptismal and marriage records, Father? And perhaps even your Communion and Confirmation records?"

"That will be quite an order, Father but we'll do it. When did this man say he was born?"

"He said he was thirty years old."

"Bien. We'll let you know."

I also called St. Tiribius' and spoke to Father Gadger. He grunted appreciatively when I told him of my suspicion that La Tour had either never been baptized or was deliberately concealing the true place of his baptism, perhaps because a previous marriage might have been noted on the register.

"Could you possibly make some fuller inquiries around the neighborhood?" I pleaded. "Could you question some people who might know this La Tour, might know his background?"

Father Gadger was smooth but firm. "He's only lived here a couple of years, Father. We don't know him in the rectory and have never seen him at church affairs. I don't know what else we can do since you don't have time for banns. Why don't you call his landlord? Maybe you could get something out of him. I'm glad I don't have this case in my lap."

That was all the help I received from Father Gadger but I could hardly expect more. However, after a moment's thought, I called information and obtained the landlord's number.

A gruff voice answered the phone. I identified myself and asked how long Mr. La Tour had lived there.

The man was respectful when he heard I was a priest.

"About two years," he said.

"Did you ever hear that he was married?"

"No, he's a single man."

"Did he ever mention or did you ever hear anyone say that he had been previously married?"

"No, Father, no. I hardly ever speak to him. I mind my own business. What's wrong? Is he in trouble?"

I laughed as gaily as I could manage. "No trouble at all. I'm just making a routine check. Thank you very much."

Although I felt a definite suspicion about La Tour, I began to wonder if I was not being overscrupulous in my concern about this marriage. After all, one could not obtain absolute certainty in these matters. If the man produced the Church-required documents, it was not necessary for me to go sleuthing all over the diocese to try to prove him false. Self-doubt made me inactive for an hour.

At the end of that time I had devised another plan. La Tour, in answer to one of my questions, had said that he had received his First Holy Communion and Confirmation in St. Lawrence's Church (on the far side of town) when he was ten years old, in other words, twenty years previously. Surely, I reasoned, St. Lawrence's priests must have demanded some proof of baptism before permitting these sacraments. It followed, then, that they might have some such baptismal information entered in their Communion and Confirmation records. I called the rectory.

"No First Communion records were kept at that time, Father," the parish secretary told me. "When was the man confirmed?"

"Twenty years ago."

"I'll call you back, Father."

I tried to read my Office for a half hour, but my attention, never too good, was extremely poor. I could not repeat to myself a word of what I had read or summarize a thought. Disturbed as I was, this disturbed me more. My nerves tightened another notch or two.

The phone rang.

"I looked five years before the date you gave and five years after," the secretary said. "There's no one by the name of 'La Tour' listed in that whole period."

I hung up eagerly. Now I was making progress! If La Tour had lied to me about his Confirmation, presumably he would not have hesitated to lie about his baptism. I decided to call him at his office, but before I could do so, I was called down to the parlor.

A pimply adolescent in blue jeans and a checked shirt leaned laconically against the doorpost, a long white envelope in his hand. He was chewing gum, naturally.

"Mr. La Tour sent this over. He wanted me to give it to you personal."

"Personally. Thank you."

The boy shrugged and clacked out, the steel clips on his shoes beating against the Pastor's parquet floors. I quickly opened the envelope and read the affidavit:

"We, Mr. and Mrs. Thomas Crasula, do solemnly swear that we are old friends of Mr. Peter La Tour and of his family and that we were present at his baptism thirty years ago in St. Joan's Church in this City. Mr. La Tour has never been married before and is now free to marry."

The statement was signed and notarized. I walked slowly up to my room. What more could I demand? Such a document was acceptable normally when parish records had been destroyed. Could I insist on anything more in this particular case? At least, I told myself, I will make him clear up the Confirmation matter.

The Pastor's door was open as I passed. On an impulse I knocked and entered the room. He was sitting on a carved high-backed chair near the window, a beautifully bound book in his hands. He was attired in an expensive-looking dressing gown of softly glowing maroon material, which contrasted with the pallor of his face. As he raised his pale, expressionless eyes to mine, he seemed like a handsome bishop, almost burned out by lifetime effort, but still able to sit out the remaining years with dignity. When you saw this almost invalid figure of a man not yet sixty, it was

82

hard to realize that Pope Pius XI was then about eighty — a dynamic fountain of world-wide activity.

I explained my problem and he listened gravely, judicially, his hands pressed together in church-steeple fashion. He stared at the hand-carved crucifix on the wall. He was like a scholar-saint, a man of wisdom above the rough and ready give and take, an oracle who might be approached for inspired solutions or sublime interpretations.

"We cannot help at times, Father," he said at last, "encountering a *casus complexus,* and when that is so, having sought counsel, we should proceed to do whatever we judge best in the circumstances, not worrying about the consequences. Having said that much, I must now add that there have been very few complex cases in my life which have not eventually given way to a solution when effort and concentration were prolonged. Of course, here you are working against time; this is an unfortunate corner in which you have allowed yourself to be boxed."

There was the slightest tinge of reproof in the last words. I saw the oracular lips move again.

"Why don't you go to the phone now — you can use mine — and call Mr. La Tour for an explanation of his unsubstantiated statement about Confirmation?"

Surprised at the dynamic nature of this advice I seated myself at the huge mahogany desk and dialed the number. The top of the desk was beautifully decorated with blotter, lamp, pen stand, clock, ash tray, leather folder. There was not a single letter or scrap of paper on the entire surface.

Suavely, I described to La Tour the report I had received about his Confirmation record.

He was silent for a moment; there was an embarrassed laugh. I could picture a slight reddish tinge creeping up his handsomely barbered neckline — I felt a certain righteous pleasure.

"I must have been mistaken, Father," he said. "I thought

I had been confirmed in St. Lawrence's. Perhaps it was in some other parish, but I was almost certain . . ."

"What other parishes did you live in?"

"Oh, we moved around a lot. And then of course I might have been confirmed in some neighboring church and not in my parish church at all."

The pastor whispered dramatically, "Ask him about his school. What grammar school did he attend?"

I asked the question.

"I was in a number of schools."

"Catholic schools?"

"Only one — St. Benedict's — and for just the final year of grammar school. I would have been confirmed by that time. It's too bad, Father; I'm sorry I misled you — unintentionally. But surely the question of a confirmation certificate cannot have any bearing on our getting married tomorrow."

"I wanted to get the facts straightened out, Mr. La Tour. It's desirable to have the certificate. Will you give it some further thought, please?"

"If you wish."

I hung up the receiver and swiveled around toward Monsignor Haggerty. I told him what La Tour had said.

He clapped his hands gracefully. "I think you have the necessary lead. Call St. Benedict's School and ask for the nun who has taught there longest. She'll probably remember this young man; perhaps they'll have some records. The *casus perplexus* will be resolved; I am sure of it."

I thanked him. As I left, he was looking wistfully toward the bedroom. Once more I stationed myself behind my telephone and, having looked up the number of St. Benedict's School, put through my call.

A female voice answered — the voice of a nun.

I asked for the Sister who had been on the faculty longest, explaining that I wanted some information on a graduate who had been in the eighth grade sixteen years previously.

"I have been here thirty years, Father," the angelic voice said. "I'm Sister Mary Agnes, presently the principal." She laughed the little laugh that nuns reserve for priests.

"The name of the former student is Peter La Tour."

There was a pause, pregnant. She spoke slowly. "I remember a Peter La Tour very well, Father. I taught him in my first year here, in the eighth grade. He was very handsome and always well dressed and polite — a little shy perhaps. But that couldn't be the one you want — that was thirty years ago."

"It certainly is an excellent description except for the shyness. Could there have been two boys by the same name — cousins perhaps?"

"Possibly, Father, but I'm sure only one Peter La Tour has graduated from this school since I have been here."

I paused. I was beginning to understand. "Did you keep records, Sister? Can you look up the name of his parents and his baptismal information?"

"Certainly, Father. Is he in trouble?"

"Not yet, Sister."

She called me back in ten minutes and confirmed my guess. Peter La Tour, the one and only, had graduated from grammar school thirty years ago. The baptismal file, Sister Mary Agnes informed me, indicated that he had been baptized in St. Etheldreda's Church forty-three years ago. The motive for La Tour's lies was now obvious, although pathetic. He could not be sure that a girl twenty-two would marry a man twice her age.

Checking with St. Etheldreda's I found that they had the baptismal record and no record of any previous marriage by Peter La Tour.

On the phone again, I said, "La Tour, if you want to be married here tomorrow, you had better get over here to the rectory in ten minutes. You have a lot of explaining ahead of you."

I hung up. The irritation had begun to agitate my system. The glands were at work. The boldness, the cold calculated effrontery of the man! And what a deception to impose on such a lovely, innocent girl as Regina! Then my outraged gallantry overflowed. For a moment, I actually considered giving the blackguard a beating.

By the time he arrived — half an hour later, I had recovered most of my suavity. Immediately, briefly, I told him what I had discovered.

He paled for half a minute, and then smiled and sank into the nearest chair. Unabashed he pulled out a cigarette.

"No smoking. The Pastor doesn't allow it."

He crumpled the cigarette.

"You have to understand, Father. Her parents have been against me from the beginning. My age might have tipped the scales against me; I couldn't take a chance on Regina's finding out my true age. She would have seen the baptismal certificate. Or you would have mentioned my age to her in your instruction. Somehow it would have been made known. I could not risk it. You see, don't you? Was that so terrible?"

"You lied under oath."

At this he bowed his head. "I know. There I was wrong, but I could not see any other way."

"You must tell Regina the truth. She has a right to know."

"But why? Is this so important?"

"You thought it important enough to conceal. I won't marry you unless you tell her the truth."

He began to cry at this point — a disgusting performance for a man of the world. I hoped madly Regina would return his ring.

But no. She called me later in the day.

"Peter has explained everything, Father. I'm sorry for what he did, what he said, particularly under oath. I'm terribly upset, so embarrassed. I'm sorry you were inconvenienced, Father."

86

"Then," I began, "then you're not going through with the marriage."

She actually laughed. "Of course, Father. I love the man. It wouldn't matter if he were fifty-three. I want to marry him."

I felt sorry for Regina, beautiful, naïve, wholesome, when I performed the simple ceremony the next afternoon. What a waste of a glorious girl on a first-class hound!

Six months later I felt sorry for La Tour and even more sorry for myself. The pure and glorious Regina had been married quietly while on a trip to Havana when she was eighteen years old. She had faked all the papers to fool the native priest about her identity, her baptism, her address. I would never have known the truth if her real husband had not sent me a letter. It seems he was the jealous type.

CHAPTER VI

I HAD no real desire to teach school. In fact I had always considered my vocation to lie in parish activity. In deciding between becoming a religious or a diocesan priest, I had been partly influenced by the desire to avoid a teaching career. For years after ordination I had feared that I might be assigned to the faculty of one of the diocesan high schools. Naturally this event came about. Such irony has been consistent in my life — perhaps in everyone's life. In any case, I found myself an English and religion teacher in the Archbishop Battle High School — and liking it rather well after the breaking-in period was over.

As I knew there was nothing I could or should do about the assignment, I just tried to make the best of it, and was pleasantly surprised. This irony too has plagued, or rather helped me. Someone asked me the other day, "Which of your many assignments did you like best?" I couldn't answer. I simply said, "I plunged into whatever I had and I was quite happy everywhere."

I think the gentleman who received this reply thought I was a rather simple type who wouldn't know a problem if I saw one. Perhaps he was right, although one's answer really depends on one's definition of happiness. On thinking it over perhaps I should have given my questioner a waggish answer. "I've been equally miserable whatever my assignment." I could have gained in prestige by such a reply.

So many odd things happen in a high school that one is hard put to select the most interesting. But let me try to tell you of my tussle with Robert Bonzer, senior extraordinary.

In my third year at Battle, I was assigned to teach, among other units, a senior class in religion. The forty boys, upon inspection, seemed average enough taken as a group. I knew from past records that several of them were intellectually brilliant. Bonzer, a recent transfer from a public school, was one of this elite number.

Quite casually he interrupted me in my opening remarks to the class.

"You mention God," he said. "How do we know there is a God? Are Catholics asked to presume as true the most important principle of religion?"

I leaned back against the freshly washed blackboard and stared at him.

He was a handsome boy with blond, wavy hair, regular features, and a poised posture unusual in a teen-ager. He seemed to be dressed exactly in the most effective way, bluish sports coat and gray tie, gray slacks. I remember the outfit well, since I saw it frequently thereafter. There was only one defect in his appearance, a slight cast in the right eye — that and small, closely fitted ears.

I decided to treat the interruption lightly.

"You must be new around here."

"Public school, but I went to catechism. I've read books."

"You'll get the proofs later on. In Catholic school you don't interrupt the teacher without raising your hand."

He mumbled something out of the side of his mouth. My pulse picked up tempo. "What did you say?"

"I said: 'That's one way of concealing ignorance.'" He didn't seem afraid; there was open contempt in his tone.

I thought of hitting him, detaining him, sending him to the principal's office. The first and last expedients would merely prove his point.

"I'm not used to taking insolence," I said.

"You weren't supposed to hear it. You asked me to repeat it."

I swallowed a large glob of anger. "Report here after school. We'll talk it over then."

I went on with the explanation, but my voice had a hurt, defensive quality which I could not eliminate. Here was a kid to be got rid of.

He was on my mind all day.

At lunch with a dozen of the other Fathers, I would have brought up my problem case but I had resolved not to talk shop at mealtimes. Actually there was no opportunity because the conversation was divided between baseball and football. One of the priests who was a friend of the priest in charge of athletics — and therefore close to the sporting world — gave us a run-down on the emerging football team. It seemed that a boy named Poganski was the one to watch.

"Good student, and drops into chapel often, too."

We all felt gratified at this information and looked admiringly at the priest who was the possessor of such vital intelligence. A good man to know.

I toyed with my lima beans and tried to think of what I would say to young Bonzer. I knew that my job was to convert not to cow. I would be fatherly, sympathetic.

I was — as always — weary when the final bell rang at three o'clock. I felt the need of a smoke, a shower, and a sleep and not of a troublesome senior. Bravely, I sat at the desk and waited for him.

He marched in briskly ten minutes later.

"You're late."

"Sorry. This is a big school. I'm new here. It takes a while to get from one classroom to another."

Always he had an answer — seemingly reasonable.

"Maybe you're in the wrong school, Bonzer." My fatherly attitude had evaporated after five minutes' waiting. "This is a school for Catholic boys — boys who believe in God, who know how to speak respectfully to teachers and priests."

He grinned boldly, his American-boy face slightly flushed.

"You're making a big deal, an opera out of nothing, Father. I thought I asked an intelligent question. These things aren't taken for granted outside. I know. I was actually doing the class a service by bringing up the question of God's existence. It's something they should hear discussed, know reasons for. How do you know what's bothering us if we don't ask questions?"

"It's not that, Bonzer. Everything in good time; we're going to prove God's existence in the second term. It was your manner — insolent — and the phrasing of the question — very provoking."

"That's the way it was in public school. The teacher expected it, didn't mind. It was more democratic, I guess."

"Nonsense. Rudeness cannot be tolerated in a classroom. It has nothing to do with being democratic."

"But why stifle honest expression of ideas or difficulties? Is this good education? John Dewey says no."

Always he had an answer.

"What do you know about John Dewey?" I demanded. "And besides he's not our favorite educator around here."

He smiled and brushed a blond hair off his shoulder. "I can see that."

I was getting too angry. I remembered fatherliness.

"Now, look here, Bonzer, I want to help you, not argue with you. Are you really worried about the existence of God?"

He stared at me for a moment, the cast giving his gaze a disturbing quality. Then he looked away and his face softened.

91

"I have problems, Father, but that's not one of them. I just wanted to bring out a point."

My fatherliness was dominant now. I lowered my voice. "Would you care to discuss these problems of which you speak? Can I help you in any way?"

He hesitated a moment, staring at the floor. "Not right now, Father. Maybe some other time. May I go now?"

I felt almost sorry for him, an intelligent, fine-looking boy with hidden problems eating away at him. "You may go," I said softly.

Calmly, happily, I rode upstairs on the elevator to the top floor where the residence quarters were located. For the thousandth time my eyes swept across the bright, modernly furnished room which had been my home for two years. Contentedly I pulled down the covers on the bed, removed my shoes and cassock and lay down for my nap. Since I had been assigned to teaching, the ritual had become habitual. I had found that without a siesta, I was hopelessly muddled for paperwork or reading in the evening. An hour's nap gave me a fresh start for the rest of the day. I thought to myself as I drifted into sleep: There are worse things than being a teacher.

I was awakened by the telephone bell. I should have told the switchboard operator not to disturb me, but I did not want it known that I took a nap. That was something to keep secret from a critical office staff who would consider it another indication of the self-indulgence of twentieth-century priests.

It was my colleague, Father Harry, on the wire.

"I don't suppose you'd want a game of handball?"

"Well, I was taking a . . ."

"You wouldn't want to have a game and go out for dinner afterward?"

"If you feel . . ."

"I didn't think you'd be in the mood. It isn't too good a time for it anyway. The courts will probably be all taken

And it looks as though it will start raining before dinnertime. Well, thanks. See you."

It is clear that Father Harry would not have made a very good salesman.

I slumped with relief back upon my well-worn mattress. The phone rang again.

It was a boy's voice. "Father Roland?"

"Speaking."

"I just want to warn you, Father, to watch out for that boy Bonzer. He's a troublemaker; he'll cause a lot of trouble in the school and get plenty of other boys in trouble."

"Who are you?" I demanded.

"I don't want to say, Father, but I know this Bonzer kid from way back. I'm warning you, Father. Give him the heave ho while you've got a chance."

"But you can't anonymously accuse . . ."

My reply was interrupted by the clicking of the boy's receiver.

I sat for a moment thinking. I knew that I could not base any positive action on a call like this. I could only decide to watch Bonzer carefully, a course I had already laid out for myself. On the morrow I would check with the office for more details of the lad's background. That was all I could do for the time being. Once again I dropped into bed.

The next day I looked in on Miss Norris, the school secretary. She was a small woman, with a large flock of odd hair. Some of us were convinced that she wore a wig. Although she was certainly on the far side of fifty, she adopted a coy attitude toward the priests of the faculty. But, in her way, she was efficient, and could even be stubborn where a school rule was at stake.

She looked up from the record card on which she was entering notations.

"How fat you're getting, Father Roland. We'll be calling you Fatsy soon, if you keep it up."

You see what I mean about being coy. Always the woman embarrassed me.

She turned stubborn when I asked for records on Bonzer.

"You'll have to ask the principal. We never give personal records without top authorization. You ought to know that by now, Father Roland. It's been policy for years. Where on earth have you been?"

I chose to ignore her piffle.

I simply said: "It's strange that a priest on the faculty — or any faculty member — should have to get special permission to see the student records. It smacks of authoritarian bureaucratism."

I stalked off toward the principal's office. I knew that eventually my remark would be reported to him. I had made it with that in mind.

Monsignor Carey, diminutive and deceptively mild, readily granted permission.

"Do you recall any special circumstances connected with admitting this boy Bonzer?" I asked.

He swung his key chain around his forefinger and gazed pensively at the rug.

"No," he said faintly. "There are so many, you know. Let's see. Bonzer? A transfer to senior year from public school? Yes. A handsome boy, brilliant record. His mother came in — rather seedy looking — said it was his own idea — he wanted at least one year of Catholic education. I said it was too bad he hadn't had a great deal more, but I'd let him in. He was very grateful, a mature boy. You'll be patient, I know. It's all so new to him."

All the while the key chain whirled.

I nodded, murmured thanks, and went to the file room. The record card showed brilliant averages. There were no character entries.

The days and weeks went by. Bonzer continued to ask questions, often pointed, but his tone was better. I could

94

still detect a shade of insolence, but not enough to supply the basis for a showdown. He seemed popular with the other boys. They were often knotted about him when I entered the room.

His quizzes indicated great intelligence and accuracy. He rarely scored under ninety-five. Frequently he brought advanced books with him to school. I would see them resting on his desk: *Great Concert Music, The Collected Poems of John Keats, The Meaning of Modern Science, The Life and Thought of Hegel.*

I had encountered bright seniors before but never one who indicated such breadth, such general cultural interest, although I admit some of the titles (like the last) made me nervous. I knew that he might have been faking, pretending to an intellectual level he did not have, merely to impress his fellows and possibly the faculty. But although I felt he was posing to some extent, I could not doubt that he had a real interest in things of the mind. His questions often indicated his reading. "George Bernard Shaw says in his preface to St. Joan such and such. What do you say about that?" Or "William James makes this or that point in *Varieties of Religious Experience.* How do you answer that objection?"

He kept me on the defensive always. Other bright students in the class began to join in, coming up with quotes, demanding extended explanations of points of doctrine. There was no chance of getting away with a superficial presentation of the religion course. It was stimulating in a way but taxing too, and of course we moved very slowly through the six-hundred-page book. In high school the teacher is obliged to cover the text from beginning to end; he has to "do" so many pages a day. Administration expects this; examinations demand it. This had always been a handicap to me; now it had become a cause of nervousness. Yet I could not bring myself to cut off questions if they were related to the matter. I think that the defensive position into which I had been maneuvered made me overeager to appear democratic in this regard. I had been trapped by my own sensitivity — something which has happened to me many times.

Three months passed in this manner. I began to hate to walk into that class to face that handsome countenance with its half-cynical smile, and to strain my mind against a flock of his supporters, eager to press the priest to the wall. So it seemed.

One day late in the term, Lipeoni, a bright-looking lad of Italian extraction, asked to see me after school. At three he came and sat beside my desk. He was typical of the good-looking, dark type of boy, with slick hair and natty clothes, but with a very human and trusting manner in dealing with a priest. I saw this type again and again during my teaching years, and I think them my favorite boys. They are knowing yet essentially innocent, respectful yet full of informal warmth, with both humor and affection in their eyes, and unfortunately just a trace of instability in their emotions. They are all life, vitality, expressiveness. I suppose they delighted me in part because of my own reserve and sobriety. The fact of being alive seemed to mean more to them than it ever had meant to me.

He was smiling but pale and his voice trembled. At first he made no sense, but then his trouble came streaming out in a flood of words, lapping one over the other, tinged with all the shades of the emotional spectrum, salted at last with unaccustomed tears.

"And so now she tells me that she's going to have a baby." The whole banal story was summed up in those words. "What'll I do, Father? What can I do?"

"How old are you?"

"Seventeen — eighteen in July."

"The girl?"

"Seventeen next month."

"How long have you known her?"

"Over a year. She's a decent girl. It was my fault."

"Would you like to marry this girl? Do you love her in that way? You don't have to marry her."

"I'd like to. We were talking about it before — before this happened. We planned to wait a year or so."

"It might be arranged — quietly. You graduate in a few months. You'll have to get a job right away and you'll have a wife and family to support for the rest of your life. Are you sure you're prepared for that?"

His eyes were aglow now with fresh hope, eagerness. He nodded emphatically.

I looked at him. He struck me as a decent boy, a good product of Catholic training.

"Why did you do it? Why did you corrupt the girl you claim to love?"

The eyes clouded, filled. The head bent.

"It was my fault; I never did anything like that before. But I'd been hearing a lot of stuff about the sixth commandment being outmoded, that it was an old taboo put in by Jews who were jealous of their women. Just that day a guy with ideas — he's read a lot — was trying to prove to me that the Church's teaching on sex was unnatural, psychologically bad, impossible. I said to him, 'Listen, Bonzer, I don't go for that talk,' but it stuck in my mind and I got into a sort of mood where I didn't know what was right, and then — you know the rest."

Bonzer. The name had slipped out. The boy continued talking, giving no sign that he realized his revelation.

At the end I promised to discuss the possible quiet marriage with the families. He need not worry, I said. If the pregnancy became noticeable before graduation, I could easily send the girl away to the country until they were ready to reveal their marriage. If they decided not to get married, I could arrange to send her to a Catholic institution where she could have the child without scandal. If necessary, even adoption could be quietly arranged. These things could be handled discreetly and with a minimum of trouble nowadays.

He was all alive again as he left. He said he was on his way to confession. Every day there was a confessor available in the chapel for an hour after school.

Bonzer. Now I had a real problem. It seemed to me at first that he would have to go. He was deliberately corrupting his fellow students. He had deceived me in a sense; I had thought that he was not really dangerous, just provocative. I had even felt that my answers were beginning to satisfy his questioning mind. Together with his other qualities, he was a good actor, it seemed. But could I still save him? Was it worth the risk to the other students for the next five months?

I decided to visit him at home, to make known to his parents what was happening, to see what his room was like, his books, to press him and his family for more details of his background. Perhaps then I would know how to help him, or perhaps I could then recommend his dismissal with an easy conscience.

I could not afford to delay. Every passing day could mean a new dose of mental poisoning for one or more of his classmates.

I went up for my nap, and the phone rang.

"Father Roland?"

It was an authoritative female voice.

"I'm Mrs. Singer. You teach my son, Walter. Now I have a complaint, Father, and a very serious one. My son's faith is being seriously threatened — in a Catholic school, no less!"

"Whhhat?"

"Did I wake you up? Sorry. A nap is one of the pre-requisites of teaching. I know. I taught for years in public school. But this boy, Bonzer, has to be stopped, Father. I'm saying this for the good of the school, not just for my son. This Bonzer ridicules the Church and priests every chance he gets. Just yesterday he said to Walter, and I quote: 'The priests use the poor-box money to gamble in the market; the communists are the only ones who really care about the poor.' He says he met an ex-priest who told him about it — a lot of other things too. That isn't so, is it Father? About the poor-box money?"

"Of course not."

"You'll know what to do, Father. Walter's all upset. I'll leave it to you."

"Yes. Thank you."

Evidence. More evidence. I hung up the phone and slumped into my chair. My nerves were tight and I longed to be rid of the whole problem. I tried to read but could not concentrate. During dinner I was abnormally quiet and could not eat much. I kept looking at my watch, desperately anxious to confront Bonzer in his own home.

At last, around eight that evening, I arrived before the old brownstone house in a middle-class neighborhood. Mrs. Bonzer, a motherly lady of fifty, answered my ring.

As she invited me into the cheerful living room she told me that Robert was at a meeting of his "study club."

"And Mr. Bonzer?"

There was a slight spasm across her face. "Mr. Bonzer passed away two years ago. A sudden heart attack. How nice of you to call on us. I do so love Catholic schooling. My husband had a prejudice against it, but I was so happy when Robert expressed the desire to go for his senior year. He needs that influence. He is brilliant but he needs guidance. He gets strange ideas at times. Advanced, I suppose you'd say. All he needs is proper guidance. But he has to look up to you. He worshiped his father but I'm afraid I'm not his mental equal. Often he is beyond me although sometimes I have to correct him."

I studied the pattern on the Turkish carpet for a few moments.

"Mrs. Bonzer," I said, "did your late husband also have what you call 'advanced ideas'?"

Again the momentary spasm.

"Well," she said slowly, "he was not quite orthodox. An intellectual and something of a rebel. No, he was not a communist, but he had a sympathy toward the Left if you know what I mean. I think often he would say things just to let off steam, you understand. He liked to shock others. Robert is a little bit the same way."

We continued for a while. When I told her what I had learned of Robert's influence on other boys, she grew pale and her lips trembled, although she did not weep as I had expected.

"I feared this, Father. I feared it so terribly. This study club has destroyed his faith."

She repeated these lines several times. At last I asked for details about the club.

She knew surprisingly little, except that it was run by a former teacher of Robert's for teen-age boys and girls to discuss current events, social problems, modern history. The teacher, a Mr. Warren, was a very charming man. She had met him on one occasion. But she was afraid he might lean a little too far to the Left. Too liberal, should she say? From what Robert told her, many of Mr. Warren's ideas paralleled those of the late Mr. Bonzer. Even more liberal, perhaps.

I reached for my hat and asked for the address of the study club. I had decided on what was — for me — an extremely bold course of action.

After reassuring Mrs. Bonzer that we would discuss the matter further before any final decision was made by the school, I hastened on foot across town to Warren's apartment where the meetings were held.

I was excited and was breathing quickly. L'affaire Bonzer had taken on great proportions for me; it had for the moment the drama of a spy hunt, although all the while I knew that, at the end, I was going to be left with a messy problem. However, for a few moments I enjoyed my investigative role.

My enjoyment ceased when I tried to formulate a plan of action. What would I do on arrival at the meeting? Should I simply walk in and ask for an explanation? Should I try to slip in unnoticed and eavesdrop for as long as necessary to obtain evidence of subversion? Should I ring the bell and simply ask for Bonzer, and then walk home with him while I made my accusations?

The last course seemed the least absurd and the most likely to succeed. Of course, while in the apartment — if they allowed me in — I would observe and absorb all possible evidence. I debated removing my Roman collar, but decided against such a course.

The apartment was on the second floor of a low-class housing project. I walked up the trash-laden stairs and pressed the buzzer at 2-E. I could smell the sickening pungence of fried shrimps in the hall. From somewhere came the blare of a radio. The door opened, on a chain. The pimply face of a teen-age girl peered out at me.

"May I come in?" I said, "I'm Father Roland. I'd like to see Robert Bonzer. His mother told me he was here."

She hesitated, looking undecided. At last: "I'm sorry, sir, but we're not allowed to admit strangers."

"Who told you that?"

"Mr. Warren."

"Do you mean there is some reason why Mr. Warren doesn't want a priest to enter the apartment? What is going on in there, that a priest can't be admitted?"

"Nothing but a meeting, sir." Her voice had begun to tremble because of my vehemence. "Just a moment, sir, I'll have to ask Mr. Warren."

She left the door ajar and in the brief moment she was gone, I heard a cultivated — almost effeminate — voice refer to "the marvelous historical insight of Karl Marx." Then I heard whispers and the pimply face was back at the door.

"Bob Bonzer will be with you in a minute, sir. Mr. Warren would like to meet you but he's in the middle of a lecture. He says he'd be happy to send you an invitation to the next meeting if you'd care to attend."

I snorted pontifically.

In a moment Bonzer appeared, his cheeks a bright red, his mouth tight. I sensed that he was both angry and afraid.

Without saying good night to the girl, he walked ahead of me down the stairs, whistling insolently.

As we gained the street, I drew up beside him. It was a cool, still night. Under other circumstances I could have enjoyed the walk through the semibright city streets, dancing as they were with unexpected shadows, half-muffled voices brushing from time to time across your eardrums, the bright eyes of lonely cars moving sometimes tentatively, sometimes boldly down deserted thoroughfares.

I told Bonzer of the charges against him, of my own suspicions of the study club.

He hummed — still insolently — as I talked.

I finished what I had to say, and he stopped short and shrugged his shoulders.

"If that's all you've got to say, Father, I'll go back to the meeting."

"Have you no explanation? No regrets? No desire to break out of this mental strait jacket you're in?"

He jutted his chin. "You should talk about mental strait jackets!"

I grabbed him by the shoulder. "Do you admit or deny the charges against you?"

He brushed my hand away. "What difference does it make? I'm out of school, either way. Right? You couldn't keep me in now, even if you wanted to. Corrupting other boys and all that. Expellable offense in any Catholic school. Right?"

"I have no doubt of it, but the principal will have to decide that."

I thought to myself that this was an impossible dilemma. If we kept him he'd continue to infect other students. If we expelled him, he's do the same somewhere else, in some public school — in addition to the fact that any good influence we might possibly exert upon him would then be completely lost.

He turned and began to walk back toward Warren's apartment.

Over his shoulder he said, "Tell Monsignor Carey to send my record to the school I came from. I'll finish the year there."

At a loss, angry, I called into the night, "You've got to try to find the truth. You can't turn your back on Jesus Christ."

I heard him snort and saw him quicken his pace back through the shadowy streets. Suddenly he began to run.

Despondent, I decided to walk off the unpleasant emotions connected with this extraordinary evening.

I blamed myself in part for this boy's condition. Had I dealt with him differently, given him more personal attention, been the wise and holy priest I should have been, then surely. . . . This sort of thinking has often come to me in the priesthood; I imagine it is the experience of everyone who has moral or spiritual charge of others. It is good for the humility but carried on too long it can be fruitless, leading to a sort of despair and a type of unhappy bitterness toward self. It can also flow from an overestimation of self, a failure to realize that, even at our best, we cannot control the wills of other human beings. There is no automatic, mechanical means of making others do good and avoid evil. We must be the best possible occasions of grace by teaching and by example, but even so the object of our attention is not forced. Even God's grace is subject to refusal. This seems terribly obvious as I write it, but I rediscovered its meaning on the meandering night walk, out of the pain of what I felt to be a personal failure. At last I told myself that I had done what was reasonable and still intended to do more; in fact I resolved to write to this boy, to try to see him again and again. But as I approached the school a generalization was forming in my mind that I had been and was, not just in this case, a mediocre priest. I was heavy-hearted as I dug for my keys.

He was standing in the shadows of the doorway, leaning against the wall, his arms folded.

We stood in the hallway and he talked quickly, quietly with just the slightest tremor in his voice.

"You win, Father. It sounds corny but you were right — I can't turn my back on Jesus Christ, although I've been fighting Him these last three months. I never had to fight Him before because I never really knew Him before I came here — except as an abstraction. I was urged to come here by Warren — planted is the word. It was an exciting idea, flattering to be chosen as the opening wedge of the Party among students in a Catholic school. I thought I was doing pretty well too, winning friends, influencing people, and all the time I was being changed. I wouldn't admit it to myself, of course. It took our little street scene tonight to bring it out into the open. There it is, Father. . . . You don't happen to have a confessional stole with you, do you?"

For a moment I hesitated. Was this perhaps a well-prepared act designed to obtain an eventual diploma from the school? A car with bright headlights passed and for the first time I saw the tears glistening in his eyes.

"Wait a minute," I said. "I'll be right back."

CHAPTER VII

TWO YEARS later when I was transferred from the high school to the staff of the Cathedral, there were those in the diocese who said that the Bishop had confused me with another priest of the same name. This was not true; the Bishop was too keen a man to make such an elementary mistake. However, I must confess that I have never fully understood why I was chosen from the mass of clergy for such a lofty post. One of my friends suggested at the time the possibility that His Excellency had heard a brief sermon which I had delivered over a local radio station. The sermon happened to be much better than my usual quality and for once my voice was not hoarse. The Bishop was known to make up his mind quickly, even suddenly, on the matter of Cathedral appointments. In any case, once more I hired a trucker to move my baggage and my books — this time to the rather solemn surroundings of the ancient Cathedral rectory.

I shall not describe my adjustment to this new life, but the transition period was emotionally, psychologically difficult, particularly after several years of teaching teen-age boys. The huge Gothic pile was in the middle of a busy section of the city and the rectory was the stopping-off place for persons of every type — from celebrities to bums — and for persons with every kind of problem — from contemplated suicide to contemplated entrance into the Trappists. No problem was too extreme and many of them were extremely extreme. Confessions were endless, often vastly complicated. The phone rang unceasingly and the parlor was rarely vacant. And added to all this were complex Cathedral ceremonies, often with a watchful Ordinary in attendance, and lengthy sermons which needed to be foolproof against misquotation in the public press. Despite my care in this latter duty, the largest mornirg paper succeeded on one occasion in attributing to me a most heinous heresy. I expected all sorts of indignant reactions from the Bishop, from the Apostolic Delegate, even from Rome itself. Actually the sermon stimulated no response whatsoever. I was forced to conclude the Church officials were as aware as I of the possible inaccuracy of secular reporting of sermons. The other possibility — that no one had bothered to read the report of my sermon — did not occur to me at all.

There were so many pressures and strains, such a load of daily work imposed on the shoulders of the Cathedral assistants that, not surprisingly, mild-mannered priests sometimes became unexpectedly unstable and normal courtesy occasionally gave way to a brusqueness which was all the more resented by the laity because it had been inflicted on them by a person they considered one of the leading priests of the diocese. These things, I suppose, are professional hazards. I know that, after six months, I found myself one day shouting and getting red in the face at a bum who had delayed my lunch to ask for the fare to the next city. From then on I decided to react very slowly and as mildly as possible, to re-new and re-form my motivation. I did fairly well from that point on, but my score was far from perfect, and I had to struggle against irritable impatience every day.

The other priests — four assistants and the rector — were excellent men, but tinged with the same tension which infected me so early in my tenure. The old Monsignor — he seemed old then — was under the additional strain of knowing that any day he might, or might not, be named a bishop. Although I do not believe he was an ambitious man, the uncertainty, the constant rumors must have been more disturbing than we realized. Of course, something similar was true even of the assistants because it was well known that the Cathedral was the "stable" from which the Bishop chose his appointees to offices of diocesan administration. It seemed that every time an administrative opening occurred, there was an atmosphere of uncertainty and expectancy in the house. We were always wondering who would be next, each individual, secretly, I fear, hoping that he would be the one to escape into the world of honorable normality.

All in all, it was an assignment which kept a man's nerves rigid most of the time. But the incident I want to describe was unusual even for the Cathedral.

I found myself one afternoon sitting in one of the small offices off the parlor staring in fascination at a very beautiful Russian woman who was telling me a most amazing story. Both her appearance and her narrative were striking. She might have doubled for Greta Garbo and what she was telling me might have made an effective Garbo script.

When she first came into the room, I thought that perhaps she was what we used to call simply "a nut." She approached me with a catlike tread, meanwhile glancing once or twice over her shoulder as though looking for pursuers. She closed in on me to such an extent that I sought refuge behind the desk. The previous week, having been caught off guard, I had been solidly kissed by a demented female on the Cathedral steps. I don't wish to give the impression that I was ever attractive to the opposite sex, even as "forbidden fruit," but in the Cathedral the usual rules did not apply. Like a boxer, one had to protect himself at all times.

She leaned over the desk and asked, "Do you mind if I close the door? This is very personal."

I blinked once or twice. This request presented a problem. St. Ignatius — and many others — have warned against just this sort of thing. Apart from any indelicate considerations, I had found it a better policy always to leave the door at least slightly ajar. Not only was reputation protected against malicious attack, but also this procedure seemed to help shorten interviews which otherwise might have been interminable. Psychologists perhaps could give a better explanation than I of the theory of the open door. In any case, I was committed to it.

I said, "I'll close it part way. We won't be heard if you speak in a low voice."

She sat down then and pushed back her camel-hair coat from her shoulder and began to pull off her black kid gloves finger by finger. Her clothes were good but lacking in chic. I gathered from this and from her accent that she was a Central European. I hardly expected her to be a Russian.

She leaned over the desk, speaking so low that I had to cup my ear like a deaf old man. I listened and listened with growing amazement.

"I am taking a great risk in coming here, Father," she said, "but I do not think that I am being followed at the moment . . .

"It would be well if I did not tell you my full name. Allow me to call myself Maria. I am connected with the Soviet Consulate; such a position, as you can imagine, involves being very closely watched. Everyone watches everyone else; it is almost as bad as in Russia. If it were known that I had come here, I would be sent back immediately, and possibly tortured until they discovered what I had said to you. Perhaps I would even be shot as a conspirator against the regime. Such things happen every day in Russia."

I did not smile because I knew that she spoke the truth. A slight sense of uneasiness tickled my spine. I wondered what lay ahead, and what the Russians would do to me if the "plot" was discovered. It would be an appalling preoccupation continually to expect a shot through the confessional.

"I know I am asking a lot of you, Father, but where else can I turn, whom else can I trust, who else is equipped to help me?"

"Suppose you tell me what it is all about. At the moment I'm lost."

I spoke in a flat, soothing tone. I was not yet convinced that this woman was not a nut.

She sat back on her straight chair and folded her hands with determined calm. The pleasant sunlight filtering through the white lace curtains imparted a reassuring sanity to the scene.

"It is in itself really a simple problem, but unfortunately, for Russians nothing of this kind is simple. It concerns my uncle, my mother's brother; he is here in America."

"So?"

"Yes. He left Russia just before Lenin came to power. He had been a soldier in the Russian army in the World War and had become a Roman Catholic during that period. My mother knows that he intended to come to this country. We have never heard from him; no doubt he realized it would be dangerous for us if he wrote."

"Where did he go? What city?"

"My mother thinks he planned to go to St. Louis. He had met a young officer from St. Louis during the war. The friend had invited him to come and visit if he ever got the chance. He mentioned it at home, my uncle, but at the time my mother did not take it seriously. But then after he left, she remembered it, and also the name of the officer — Lawrence Scott."

"That is probably not a common name," I said. "It shouldn't be too hard to track him down if he's still in St. Louis."

"You think so?" Her eyes grew bright.

"Who can tell? Have you any more information?"

She lowered her eyes again. "My mother thinks that he may have entered the priesthood. He had become very devout, always reading spiritual books. She has always felt that he became a priest."

I had been sitting rather tensely but now I relaxed. Here was a lead which might solve the problem in two minutes. I looked at her complacently.

"I'm afraid you'll have to give me your family name, after all. If your uncle is a priest, I can locate him in a couple of minutes by means of the *Catholic Directory*. But I must know his name."

She reached for the pad and pen on the desk and wrote "Peter Alexandrevsky."

I walked out of the little office, through the now crowded parlor, past the grim receptionist who invariably resented my spending more than five minutes with any one caller because — as she told the Rector — it crowded up the parlor so. I entered the elevator and pushed the button for the top floor. In a minute I would have the *Catholic Directory* in my hand, I thought, and perhaps this person's problem would be solved, and I could move on to someone else's problem. My quick flash of the parlor had indicated an ominously large catch of problems this sunny afternoon. That was one of the faults of sunny afternoons: people with problems took walks and eventually passed the Cathedral rectory. Thus tempted, a goodly number would enter the rectory, thinking that Cathedral priests would have ready solutions.

I pulled my *Catholic Directory* from the shelf and turned to the alphabetical listing of all the priests in the United States. It took me only a moment to discover that there was no Peter Alexandrevsky in the United States, much less in the archdiocese of St. Louis. I checked the list again. I did discover a "Pierce Alexander," and in St. Louis at that. It was a possibility, if not a good one. I wrote his name and address on a piece of paper and returned to the elevator, repeating my original safari in reverse. At last I walked into the little office. It was empty.

I saw one of her gloves on the floor, under the desk. Closing the door, I bent down and picked up this "souvenir" of the strange young woman's presence. Upon examination I found that there was a little piece of paper rolled up in the little finger of the glove. With some difficulty, I fished out the paper, unrolled it, laid it on the desk.

Suspiciously I looked over my shoulder. Should I pull down the shades? I forced a grunt at such an absurdity. The note was brief:

"Some one has come into the parlor who may or may not be dangerous. Best to leave. I shall try to come back soon. Maria."

I walked to the doorway and looked into the parlor. It seemed slightly less crowded.

"Did anyone other than the blonde woman leave?" I asked Jane, the receptionist.

"Yes, a man. He left a few seconds after she did — muttered something about not being able to wait. He seemed like a foreigner to me."

"What did he look like?"

"Odd-looking. His clothes didn't fit too well. Forty or fifty, I should say. Dark and foreign-looking."

Slowly I re-entered the parlor.

"Next, please," I said to the waiting crowd.

After an hour or so, the parlor had been cleared.

I got my hat and told Jane, "I'm going out for a little walk — ten minutes — no more. I need the air."

It was one of those pleasant fall afternoons when the light is richly golden and the air seems to lap against your skin like tepid water. The city canyons seemed glorified and the moving masses of pedestrians benign and full of well-being. But my thoughts were not happy. Maria's visit, her abrupt departure, the dark foreigner — thoughts of such things could spoil the best of days. I myself might be in danger, although I conceived of this as unlikely. Was she even now being grilled at the embassy? I had the impulse to call the police and break into the building which housed the Russian Consulate, but I knew at once that this was impossible. I felt helpless; I could do nothing but wait.

She telephoned that night.

"Are you all right?"

"Yes." Her voice was hurried, faint.

"That man?"

"I don't know. Nothing has developed. I cannot speak now. Where can we meet? Not at the rectory."

I was prepared for this. "Tomorrow evening at eight o'clock in the waiting room, third floor, of St. Ephraim's Hospital. We can pretend to strike up a casual acquaintance while waiting to see patients. From the waiting room, one can watch the elevators."

"*Merci. Au revoir.*" She hung up, leaving me with a tense stomach for the next twenty-four hours.

I arrived at the hospital at seven forty-five and sat in the third-floor waiting room, puffing furiously on a pipe and staring with unseeing eyes at the evening paper. I had told the floor nurse that I expected to meet someone at eight o'clock. It was a Catholic hospital where I was well known; no questions were asked.

Over the top of my paper I watched Maria step off the elevator. She was the only passenger for the third floor. I nodded to her and she entered the waiting room and sat down two seats away from me.

"We can talk here," I said, putting down the paper.

"One cannot be too careful." She hardly moved her lips and looked straight ahead at the opposite wall. "Suddenly the elevator may disgorge a spy, and all is lost, if we are found talking."

112

I lifted up the paper. It seemed absurd to act so oddly in the security of St. Ephraim's but I was game. It reminded me of many a movie. I toyed with the idea of putting a peephole in the middle of the paper. Instead, I told her of what I had learned from the *Catholic Directory*. I told her about "Pierce Alexander," and said that he might possibly be our man.

She seemed, naturally, disappointed. I noticed that she was better dressed tonight, like a young woman going out for a social evening — or on a visit to a sick acquaintance.

"Can you help me, Father? Can you find out more about this Reverend Pierce Alexander? I could not ask you to go to St. Louis but isn't there something that could be done?"

"I could not make such a trip at this time. I can write him a letter and simply ask him the necessary questions."

She turned her head slightly. "I would prefer to avoid correspondence, if possible. It can, unfortunately, be intercepted."

"Very well. I'll call him on the telephone."

The trim floor nurse, delightfully starched, swung through the doorway of the waiting room.

"Did you find the person you were waiting for, Father?"

She was trying to be nice, helpful. I felt rather foolish, holding a paper, with Maria two seats away.

"All's well, thanks," I said.

The nurse stood puzzled for a second, shrugged, and continued her rounds. I wondered what she thought was going on. I was consoled by the realization that nurses rarely have time to think. This can be a blessing as well as a handicap.

Maria had begun to puff Garboesquely on a long, thin cigarette.

"Will you call him, Father?"

"Now? Here?" I put aside the newspaper.

"Yes. There must be a phone booth in the hall. I have a purseful of change."

I hesitated. My sense of order was disturbed. I was not emotionally prepared for such drastic action, but rather content to permit this matter to remain in the conversational stage. Now I was about to become involved.

I pulled a slip of paper from my pocket. For a second I studied Father Alexander's name and telephone number.

"You'd better give me a handful of change. I have less than a dollar's worth."

Smiling, she scooped coins out of her purse into my cupped hands. I sincerely hoped that the nurse would not decide to look in at this point.

Suddenly I sat down again. Sense was not being made.

"Suppose it is your uncle. What do you want me to say to him?"

It seemed to me that her lips tightened and her eyes flickered slightly.

"Just tell him," she said, "that his niece wants to speak to him. Then put me on the wire."

"Suppose his phone is tapped; Mr. Stalin might get mad at you."

"I will not give my last name; I will disguise my voice. Besides, I don't think they would bother to tap his wire. What reason could they have?"

"Perhaps they know all about him. They may have been watching him a long time — just waiting for something like this." I paused. "I'm telling you? You should be an expert."

"I think I can take a chance on this."

I did not move from my seat. She pressed toward me.

"Please, Father, at least call him yourself and find out if it's he."

Her eyes were liquidly appealing; her right hand was gracefully outstretched in supplication. A youthful Garbo.

Unmoved, I jingled the money in my hands.

"What's it all about, Maria? Are you going to all this trouble to say hello to a long-lost uncle, or is there something more to it? If it's as simple as you say, why don't you simply tell them at the consulate what you want to do? Why should they object?"

I realized that the question was foolish, but I wanted to stall; I wanted clarification.

For a second her mouth hung open; then she sat primly back in her chair.

"Don't you understand, Father, that the real danger is not to me but to my uncle. If they knew about him; if they could locate him, don't you see what pressure they could put upon him — perhaps to spy, perhaps even to return to Russia? They would tell him that my mother and I, our whole family, would suffer unless he complied. Don't you see how he could be tormented for the rest of his life?"

Her primness had given way to anguished sincerity. I was truly moved, sorry that I had raised any questions. But, despite my emotion, I felt the need to re-explore one point, even though it made me seem an unfeeling brute.

"Granting your point, don't you think it would be better to leave your uncle alone? A how-do-you-do is not worth the risk we're — you're taking in this situation."

"Father, I don't think you really believe what you're saying. A priest could not be so inhuman. To ignore the existence of my mother's brother, to let him continue in ignorance of our existence, our continuing love for him, not to communicate when there is a chance to do so — Father, I trust you spoke without thinking. I appreciate so much what you have already done; I would not want to involve you in danger — although I do not think there is any likelihood of danger in your case. Please, if you want to withdraw, do not hesitate, although it would be a great misfortune for me. Will you give me the telephone number of this Father Alexander? I shall make the call myself. But I do not know what I shall do if he is not my uncle. I do so need the help of a native American."

Her eyes were filled with tears now. I felt like a crawling insect. Clerical chivalry had never fallen lower.

"Easy," I said. "I was just exploring the angles of this question. One mustn't act impulsively. I'll make the call."

With a rattle the elevator doors opened and a sheet-covered patient was wheeled into the corridor on a moving table. I reached for the newspaper and studied it eagerly until the little procession disappeared down the hall.

"Father, we had better not stay here much longer. I am so grateful."

"Right." I entered the phone booth and placed a person-to-person call to Father Pierce Alexander in St. Louis. There was some confusion at the other end of the line and then at last a voice with a definitely American accent:

"Father Alexander speaking."

I debated whether to hang up, but decided to persevere. "Father Peter Alexandrevsky?"

There was a pregnant pause.

"Is this a joke? Who is this?"

I identified myself.

"I am looking for a Father Peter Alexandrevsky and I wondered if you might be he. I have an important communication for him from someone very dear to him."

"Unfortunately, Father, my name is Pierce Alexander. Why pick on me?"

"Just the similarity of names. I thought you might have changed your name."

"A rather tenuous conclusion, I'm afraid. You haven't been celebrating, Father?"

I choked off both my anger and my embarrassment.

"No, Father Alexander, this is a very serious matter. Would you do me a favor?"

"Within reason."

"Will you look up Lawrence Scott in the St. Louis telephone directory for me."

116

"You could ask information. . . . All right, just a minute."

His voice had a highly aggrieved tone.

In a moment he was back on the line. "No luck. Any other little thing I can do for you?"

"Have you ever heard of a Lawrence Scott?"

"Never. There are about a dozen Scotts in the directory but no Lawrence Scott."

Father Alexander was very patient considering the nature of the circumstances. At my request, he dictated the first names and telephone numbers of all the Scotts in the St. Louis directory. Naturally I had to deposit more money in the coin slots. He was very patient indeed.

I returned to Maria with my list and recounted the essentials of my call. She seemed resigned.

"We must part now," I said. "I'll call everyone on this list tomorrow. This is Tuesday; try to get in touch with me by Friday. I am determined now to go through with this search even if I have to fly to St. Louis."

She nodded and whispered, "I am so terribly grateful."

"Go down the stairs and out the side exit. I'll wait a few minutes."

"Yes." The eyes began to fill again as she turned and walked to the stairway. It seemed to me that she was quite emotional for a woman who had lived all her life in Soviet Russia. She must have had a great deal to cry about, and a good chance to toughen her reactions, and yet here she was with the brimming eyes twice in the space of a half hour. Or perhaps she was putting on a show for my benefit. Greta Garbo, Junior.

Walking through the cool night back to the Cathedral rectory, I meditated on the strange role, or rather roles, of the modern priest. In the minds of the people, the priest was ordained to help them in any way they, the laity, might define. You were called on to place people in new apartments, to assist them in getting jobs, to urge them not to

117

jump off window ledges, to help their children gain admission to sometimes reluctant colleges, to advise them on the national and international situation, to help them win a strike or to lift the standard of wages, to recommend to them a psychiatrist, to join their civic committees, to give lectures on Egyptian pottery, etc., etc. — and all this in addition to what was once considered normal priestly work. And, of course, you could not refuse requests for aid, no matter how unusual. If you balked, you were met with the inevitable hurt comment, "I thought priests were supposed to be like Christ, were supposed to help people when they needed help."

"True," you replied, "but . . ." and then you realized that you could say nothing that would be really satisfactory, and if you were lucky and a little lazy, you might be able to "refer" the "case" to someone "better equipped to handle it."

And now I found myself in the middle of Russian intrigue, without much hope of referring the case to anyone but the Deity.

Surprisingly, I slept rather soundly that night although I was awakened by the alarm clock in the middle of a dream about scarred prisoners trapped without air in a salt mine, which I later presumed to have been in Siberia. The entrapment itself was not the worst feature of the dream. What disturbed me most was the vision of Maria looking through a glass-covered aperture in the roof and laughing madly. The thought of it disturbed me all during my meditation and Mass, and while eating my breakfast in the funereal rectory dining room, I began to wonder if I were not being "used" in some sinister way which I could not understand. The young priest opposite me at the table was fortunately screened by his morning paper and could not have seen the varying emotions which battled for possession of my face as I analyzed the situation from every aspect. Fortunately too, although a master of sociability on other occasions, he was always taciturn to the point of rudeness until an hour after breakfast. With the enveloping paper and the regressive mood, then, he could not know that I had almost made up my mind to fly to St. Louis on my next day off — and to fly back the same night. In the middle of my profound analysis, I had reached a moment of truth, or rather of decision. I would see the matter through to the end, hang the cost — of numerous telephone calls and a possible round-trip plane ticket to St. Louis. I rose from the table renewed, said a cheery good-by (rewarded by a grunt) to my confrere and, once in my room, moved freely toward the instrument (the telephone) which might make a dramatic flight unnecessary.

I shall not relate the details of that day of telephoning except to say that my calls were fruitless. The Scotts in the St. Louis telephone directory were not the Scotts who had friends in Russia. Until I learned by hard experience the least provocative phrasing, my questions caused some semi-explosive reactions. But toward the end I had my patter down smoothly and might even have sold some insurance — had that been my line. In short, the St. Louis trip was definitely on, and my immediate problem was simply to make another phone call to conclude arrangements. This was simple: I would arrive at ten on Thursday morning and depart at eleven the same evening. This would give me thirteen hours to find the needle. I knew I was being optimistic, but I had determined to go forward blindly, doing my best — and besides, there was always the remote possibility of persuading the Rector to grant an extra day off. This request, however, I preferred to keep in reserve.

Maria, when she called that night, seemed unsurprised either at my phone failures or my high-flown plans. She was clearly having an austere reaction to her emotional display of the previous evening.

The following morning, with many misgivings at the nebulous nature of my proposed search, I boarded the St.

Louis plane. The flight was uneventful; I read my Breviary, stared out the window, and, for part of the trip, closed my eyes and tried to rest. At this last I was not too successful because I was nervous and uneasy about the prudence of the whole enterprise. However, I had worked out a plan of action and I was determined to put it into effect.

After the shiny white plane had settled onto the sunlit St. Louis airfield, I took a taxi immediately to the diocesan chancery office. I asked the polite but puzzled young monsignor who greeted me to check the records back to "1920 or so" for a Father Peter Alexandrevsky who might have served in the diocese for some period of time. The monsignor was accommodating, as was one of his female secretaries who spent thirty minutes in this fruitless search.

My next stop was city hall and in particular the Bureau of Real Estate Assessment. Did the city have a Lawrence Scott on the tax rolls?

This question elicited a bit of grumbling from the obese clerk, but he finally agreed to make the search in the records. It took him only a few minutes to report a Lawrence Scott at 26 Cedarhurst Road.

I was, of course, elated but I would not permit myself much self-congratulation. The possibility of the wrong Lawrence Scott was always present; I adhered to my policy of prudent pessimism. I looked at my watch; it read 11:30.

At 26 Cedarhurst Road, an open-faced man of about forty opened the door in response to my ring. He welcomed me with a smile. He had just come in for lunch, he informed me. He was a surveyor.

I sat down in the pleasant living room and asked him the key question.

"You were on the Russian front in the war, Mr. Scott?"

"Yes." His lips tightened.

"You knew Peter Alexandrevsky?"

I thought a flicker of suspicion lighted his eyes.

"May I inquire why you ask that question, Father?"

I smiled. "There is no need to worry; I am not a Russian spy. His niece has been in touch with me, has asked me to try to track him down. There has been no contact since he left Russia."

"Is the niece here, in the United States?"

"Yes."

"Are you sure it is his niece?"

I hesitated just a moment. "I'm quite sure. I hope she has not been deceiving me. Why should she?"

"She may be using you. It's an old game with Russian agents. They may be trying to find Peter in order to put some sort of pressure on him either to return or to act as their tool in this country. They may threaten to persecute or even to kill his relatives in Russia if he refuses to co-operate. This would not be the first time this sort of thing had happened."

Slowly, I said, "I have no reason to doubt that the woman is sincere. After all, I think I should be a fairly good judge of human nature; I deal with a great many people every day. I can usually judge a faker."

"Usually, yes. But this woman may be a trained actress. One can't be too careful."

Instinctively I looked out the window. The street was empty.

"Father," he said, "I'm going into the next room to make a phone call. Peter will have to decide for himself."

I nodded dumbly. I was not emotionally prepared for the objections which Scott was raising.

I could hear a muffled voice in the next room; the words were not distinguishable.

Scott appeared in the doorway, his jaw hard.

"Peter wants to know if the woman mentioned any previous communication whatsoever between her or her mother and himself since he has been in this country."

"No," I said quickly. "That's just the point; she told me they haven't been in touch with him since he left Russia. They weren't even sure if he was alive."

He turned abruptly and resumed his phone conversation. Then I could hear him hanging up.

He sat beside me on the sofa.

"Father, Peter said I could tell you that he is a Brother in a religious order, that he now bears a religious name quite different from his original name and that he is eternally grateful to you for your efforts. He also asked me to tell you that he has been secretly in communication with his sister and niece in Russia on several occasions since his entrance into this country. In other words, this woman is a dangerous fraud."

I sat in a sort of daze on an early plane back. I tried not to think, but I was angry, deeply shocked, revolted. A good part of the time I prayed incoherently for the poor people of Russia.

The next evening "Maria" called on the phone. When I started to shout, the receiver at the other end clicked. I never heard from her again.

CHAPTER VIII

ONE OF the several areas of activity and responsibility of a priest connected with a cathedral parish is the apostolate of the rich. As a prelate once truly remarked, "We should never forget that rich people have souls and need help to get to heaven just as much as anyone else." The Gospels would indicate that the well endowed need unusual assistance to squeeze through the needle's eye, and the cathedral clergy are frequently called upon to lead the well-laden camel by the bridle, meanwhile lightening the load as much as feasible.

It is not difficult to understand why the wealthy tend to associate themselves with the cathedral parish of a diocese. Here they are close to the ecclesiastical nobility, headed by the bishop; here they are at the center of Catholic thought, liturgy, planning, culture; here they meet others of their own kind in a transcendent setting; here Church honors are dispensed; here, supposedly, one hears the finest singing, the finest preaching.

My own dealings with rich parishioners were varied in tone and significance. I would find it hard to generalize my experience. Some felt that I was not worth talking to because I was not a monsignor; others came to me in the most abject humility for counsel.

I remember one dowager (she had contributed heavily to the diocesan building fund) who spoke to the Cathedral priests as though their social standing were little better than that of a chauffeur or doorman. There was always an implied threat in her tone of voice . . . "Fall down and worship," it would say, "or I will report you to the Bishop, and then see what will happen to you."

Actually, only the newer priests were afraid of this lady. The veterans knew that the Bishop, although he welcomed the generosity of the laity, was not inclined to run the Church at their dictation. However, a complaint was not likely to foster peace of mind in any curate, young or old. A sort of squeeze was always on in dealings with the rich. One could not afford to ignore Church law or custom to favor a select group nor could one afford to alienate prospective or past benefactors of the diocesan works of charity. Often it was a *casus perplexus*. It was a wary priest who would not blunder occasionally.

Since my experience in the Cathedral parish I have come to have greater sympathy with Church leaders in their dealings with the wealthy. Often these leaders are accused of fawning over the proud possessors of wealth and conferring upon them special privileges in violation of St. James' injunction not to show more honor to a beringed than to a ringless worshiper. If this accusation were true and if respect of persons were the principal basis for attention, then indeed one might tremble for the state of the Church. No doubt there are occasional self-seeking and greedy ecclesiastics but there are others who are greedy only in behalf of the poor and who seek to enlist in the corporal ranks of mercy the aid of those who can be most helpful. Honors are frequently distributed, it is true, but is this a matter for censure? Is it conceivable that a great gift should be received without great gratitude and appreciation? Even the most critical observer of diocesan mores would be astounded to see a bishop receive a check of half a million dollars for the diocesan orphanage with a mere "Thank you and good night." Charity works both ways, even though an element of cynicism may enter from outside.

Reading over what I have just written, I am somewhat amused at the position I have taken. I feel justified, however. If a Bishop can encourage rich people to help poor people without sacrificing any basic Christian value, I'm in favor. I will admit, however, that the situation is not always as simple as I have described it.

In any case, I found myself very much drawn into the rich man's world when Mr. Clarence Halligan, a real-estate magnate, developed a surprising admiration for my priestly and other qualities.

The relationship began simply enough. His wife, a stout and somewhat phlegmatic lady, had a heart attack on a night when I happened to be on duty. As the result of a telephone call, I proceeded to the fashionable apartment house (owned by Halligan) where the Halligans lived and after being held up for five minutes by a doorman, who insisted on calling up the apartment to ascertain if I was admissible, I proceeded to administer the Last Sacraments to the stricken woman while Mr. Halligan looked tearfully on. It was two o'clock in the morning. As I finished, a young doctor, who had withdrawn on my arrival, re-entered the bedchamber.

Clarence Halligan, unlike his wife, was thin and nervous with a curiously indirect manner. When I left the sick room he followed me quietly and placed a hand on my shoulder.

"It isn't often, Father Boland," he said, "that we have the pleasure of a priest's company at this time of morning, but I must say that of all the times I have entertained priests, there has been no occasion when I — and I speak for my wife too — have been happier for one's presence than during this disturbing occurrence. Would you care for a drink?"

"No thank you. The name is Roland by the way."

"I once had the pleasure of having a very dear friend by that name — now dead unfortunately. He was chairman of Dutcher's Steel. Went very quickly. But how interesting — Roland Boland?"

"No, Roland is my last name."

He was ushering me down a long hall to a brightly lighted library. The carpet sank lovingly under my tired feet.

"Sit down a moment, Father Roland. I have made two or three very neat gaffs in the past week. Have you ever noticed that such things are usually grouped in a short period of time? Deals can be ruined in our business that way. Will you have a cigarette? . . . Father *Roland,* of course. I know I've heard you many times in the Cathedral. I've always enjoyed good preaching. My wife, too."

Here he sniffed and rubbed a knuckle in his eye. I noticed he was fully dressed and perfectly groomed despite the hour. I looked at the extended cigarette case and saw a fifty-dollar bill resting on top of the long, thin cigarettes.

I smiled and shook my head. "I rarely smoke cigarettes, and never green ones."

He wheezed out a laugh.

"Actually," I said, "I'm grateful, but the Bishop has requested us not to accept offerings on sick calls."

He snapped the case. "Well then, let us not depart from His Excellency's regulations. I consider myself fortunate in having met him once or twice. Both my wife and I would like so much to know him better. Margaret has been heard to speak of him as one of the greatest living Americans. However, you may find something — a token — in the mail one of these mornings."

As he spoke he was in constant motion, pacing back and forth across the rug, picking up and putting down small pieces of bric-a-brac with which the tables were generously laden. I thought that the Bishop might also like to know Halligan and, if she survived, Mrs. Halligan, a whole lot better. Whether this placed an obligation upon me, I was not certain at the time.

The youthful physician appeared at this point with a moderate yet slightly optimistic smile on his unshaved face. For a doctor, he seemed ill at ease.

"I'm hopeful, Mr. Halligan. Things may not be as bad as they first seemed."

Halligan now assumed a directness which he had not shown with me.

"What does that mean?"

"That her chances for complete recovery seem good."

"You mean it was a mild attack?"

"Comparatively, yes."

"But you'll send nurses."

"Yes. Certainly."

The doctor, whose name I never discovered, all but backed out of the room. Halligan followed him.

"Excuse me, Father," he whispered en route. "I want to hear what this medical jackanapes has to say."

It seemed almost as though he held the doctor responsible for the existence of the emergency. I decided at this point that I would not care to be on the opposite side of a real-estate table from Mr. Halligan.

He was composed, even contemplative when he returned to the huge room.

"Naturally," he said, his eyes rolled heavenward, "I am deeply gratified by the course of events. Mrs. Halligan, you know, is most pious, a frequent communicant. I know it will be a hardship for her to miss her devotions while she is confined to her bed."

"I can bring Holy Communion each day, if you wish."

He looked at me mildly, smiling sweetly. "Could you? I didn't dare to ask. I know she would find it most consoling."

Thus, for a month, I entered the Halligan apartment every

morning carrying the Sacred Host to the rich woman, who, I discovered, was a charming, jovial lady. Always Halligan met me at the door, stood by, and escorted me from the room when the sick call was complete. More than once he hinted that he intended to write to the Bishop about my "kindness" and "courtesy." Meanwhile, somewhat paradoxically, he hinted more than once at his desire to "get to know His Excellency better." Actually my contact with the Ordinary was confined for the most part to assisting him occasionally at Cathedral functions. He lived in his own private residence and might as well have resided on the moon as far as any personal relationship between him and me was concerned. He was well aware of my existence, had appointed me to my present assignment, and thought well of me as far as I could tell. Beyond this there was nothing. However, Mr. Halligan was correct in judging that I was in a good position to promote a "friendship" of the type he indicated. In acting as liaison between the Bishop and the real-estate operator I might even gain the Bishop's special and approving attention to myself — not that I considered this a legitimate objective.

I decided that I needed some sort of informal counsel from an old hand in Cathedral problems, namely the Rector, Monsignor Gavin. I was not entirely sure of the prudence of this procedure because I felt instinctively, but without any solid grounds, that Monsignor Gavin held me in mild dislike. It had been rumored that he had had someone else in mind for the opening which the Bishop had chosen me to fill. Certainly the Rector had never displayed any great warmth in his manner toward me. But our relationship was livable and overtly cordial, although sometimes at table I seemed to detect a suppressed snort from his direction when I made a pronouncement of some kind on the subject up for discussion.

About two weeks after the original sick call to Mrs. Halligan, I had the rather unusual experience of being alone at supper with the Monsignor. As we were toying with our minute steaks in comparative silence, I asked casually,

"Do you know a man named Halligan, Clarence Halligan?"

"What?"

The Rector had a trick of appearing not to hear a question on the first time around. He was not deaf but apparently used the device either to gain thinking time or to throw the questioner off balance. In any case, it was not a pleasant habit.

"Halligan, Clarence Halligan. Do you know him?"

"Everyone knows him or of him. He's one of the biggest real-estate men in the city."

He made a vicious incision in the steak. "He's never done much for the Church, though. Puts a couple of hundred in the basket at Christmas and Easter. What do you know about Clarence Halligan?"

He withdrew his eyes from the steak long enough to glance at me appraisingly, with just a shade of distaste. His tone was slightly accusing, but this was not unusual. In conversing with the Rector, one expected to be on the defensive. I studied him for a moment before I answered. His face had lost its distinctive shape long ago through fullness of cheek and overlapping jowls. Although he had a naturally spare frame, the accumulated weight of his priestly years had given him an enormous stomach which even a loose-fitting cassock was unable to hide. His eyes were large and pale brown; their appraising expression rarely changed no matter how animated or relaxed his face might be. These were eyes which had seen much, forgotten nothing, and evaluated everything. His shock of wavy hair, still black, gave him a deceptively youthful appearance from a distance; it was only at close range that you saw the lines and shadows which time and struggle had left on his countenance. He spoke rather quickly, in a somewhat higher pitch than you might expect, with a slight affectation in his vowel sounds.

"Clarence Halligan," I replied to his question, "called me to attend his wife when she had a heart attack. I still attend her. He has hinted — more than hinted — that he would be happy to be on more intimate terms with the Bishop."

He grunted through his nose. "That's not unusual. Trust the loaded laity; they gravitate toward the purple like a gull toward a fish. Let them have a little money in their pocket and they look for papal honors immediately. What does he want?"

"I don't know what he wants, if he wants anything. I presume he would just like the experience of being friendly with the Bishop. I imagine he could be very helpful to the diocese."

The Rector's frown relaxed and he thought for a moment. When he spoke again, his voice was less harsh. He seemed to have reappraised the position quickly.

"Did he say anything about how he wanted to help the diocese?"

"No."

"I imagine the Bishop would be delighted to know this man better. He doesn't have a bad marriage or anything like that, does he?"

"Not as far as I know. I doubt it."

"Well then, there doesn't seem to be any reason why he shouldn't be invited to lunch at the Bishop's house. If I were you I'd call the Bishop's secretary and arrange to see the Bishop. Tell him the story and then let him carry the ball. Ten to one he'll invite Halligan to lunch and they'll be as chummy as identical twins before you know it."

He stirred his coffee and then added, "The Bishop seems to have a way with these people. They all worship him even though it usually costs them a lot of money — and sometimes a lot of time and effort. I'm glad I'm not the Bishop — I couldn't stomach that type of socializing; I'm not built that way."

I did not argue the point, although there were those in the diocese who said that Monsignor Gavin was most likely to succeed the present Ordinary, and that he was not displeased at the prospect.

I said simply, "You don't think the Bishop would regard me as presumptuous?"

"My boy, you won't hurt yourself a bit by this little mission."

He blew his nose sonorously in a freshly ironed handkerchief and then looked at me shrewdly. "You're not gunning for something are you? Trying to go places?"

I could feel my neck blushing. Although I was not "gunning for something," I was not averse to making a favorable impression on the Ordinary.

I said "I'm not gunning, Monsignor. The situation seems to call for some sort of response. I'm just trying to do the right thing. That's why I asked your advice."

He sniffed. "Well, you've got it. Let's say Grace. In the Name of the Father . . ."

I spent some uneasy moments that night trying to make up my mind to call the Bishop's secretary. I lay awake most of the night telling myself both that I would be a fool to get involved and a fool not to get involved. I had visions of the Bishop's scornfully ordering me out of his office or, alternately, placing his paternal hand on my shoulder and saying, "I predict great things for you, Father Roland."

I was similarly distracted during meditation and Mass the following morning, so distracted that I forgot to be annoyed by the usual clatter of heels approaching the Communion rail at the Offertory. In the Cathedral, there was always a race for early position at the altar rail by those who had timed to the second their subsequent arrival at work. This was but one of many irritations the priests had to endure during the celebration of daily Mass.

Finally at ten o'clock, I called the Bishop's secretary.

"This is Father Roland; I would like to see the Bishop."

"Father who? You'll have to speak a little louder."

My nervous hoarseness had embarrassed me as usual; the "frog" never failed me during important phone calls.

"Father Roland," I almost shouted.

"Yes, what can I do for you?"

Monsignor Semple was pleasant and personable, but understandably rushed and harried. He inclined toward keeping communication at a minimum level.

"I would like to see the Bishop about what I think might be an important matter."

"The Bishop is always glad to see his priests if there is sufficient reason." A note of caution invaded his voice. "Can you give me some idea as to what the important matter is about?"

"It's about a wealthy man named Halligan who would like to become acquainted with His Excellency."

There was a pause. Then, "I'll call you back."

The phone clicked.

After ten nervous minutes, Semple called me back.

"His Excellency will see you at your convenience. That means immediately."

"I'll be right over."

I hurried into the bathroom to comb my hair. Heart pounding outrageously, I gave my shoes an unnecessary brush. Then I donned my best, or rather better, suit. It was too late to do anything about the small gravy spot on the lapel.

Essaying nonchalance, I walked casually out of the rectory and up the block to the episcopal residence. A pleasant-faced maid took my hat and escorted me into a huge Renaissance parlor where generations of bishops stared severely down on my emotional instability. Sitting stiffly on a straight-backed chair of ancient oak, I found that my hands and arms had suddenly become a problem to me. I was unable to arrange them in a position of satisfactory inevidence. I felt a little ill.

Monsignor Semple swept in, distracted, rushed.

"The Bishop will see you in his office. The end of the hall at the right."

Wobbly I walked the fifteen yards and knocked timidly.

"Come right in, Father Roland," the resonant voice called.

He did not rise from his report-laden desk when I entered, but he beckoned me to a chair near him.

"I'm sorry," he said, "that I haven't been able to get to know you better, Father Roland, although perhaps I know you better than you think." He laughed. "I try to keep my eyes open at Cathedral ceremonies. But the fact is that I'm so busy, day after day, that I haven't the time I'd like to devote to my priests."

I found myself nodding eager agreement to his every phrase.

"Monsignor Semple said you wanted to talk to me about a man named Halligan. Is that Clarence Halligan of the real-estate family?"

"Yes, Your Excellency."

His Excellency sat back, relaxed and smiling. He was a dapper little man of sixty with a fresh haircut, sparkling shoes, and a perfectly tailored cassock. His pallid face had a bland expression and his light-brown eyes were gentle.

He smiled. "He would like to become better acquainted?"

"Yes, Your Excellency."

"Invite him to lunch." He picked up his memo book with a quick, vital gesture that seemed characteristic. "Next Thursday at one. You come too."

"Oh, thank you, Your Excellency."

"I always say, and I think it's something all of us should keep in mind, that the rich as well as the poor have souls to be saved. And perhaps we can save both rich and poor by taking from one to give to the other. Don't you agree?"

I smiled and nodded eagerly. "I think you've hit the nail on the head, Your Excellency."

A shadow of annoyance blotted out the benignity of his countenance for a moment.

"That expression 'hit the nail on the head,'" he said slowly in his Eastern private school voice, "reminds me of something I wanted to mention to you, Father Roland, in connection with your sermons."

I could feel the warm flush of embarrassment.

He held up his hand in graceful deprecation. "Don't misconstrue me. I've enjoyed your talks when you've preached at the High Mass. They were well prepared, well thought out, and carefully rehearsed. I like your preaching very much; I've learned things, I must admit. I would just suggest that you take the precaution of combing your manuscripts for clichés before delivery. It's so easy to fall into them — I know. With just a little extra effort you can rid yourself of expressions like 'hit the nail on the head' and 'pass the flaming torch of truth'; I believe you used the latter expression on Catechetical Sunday."

I bowed my head miserably.

"To get back to Mr. Halligan, Father Roland. Have you any idea of what he has in mind?"

My spirits revived slightly at this. Halligan, after all, was a count in my favor even if clichés were against me.

"He didn't go into detail, Your Excellency. He's a rather indirect man in his speech, but I have the distinct impression that he is contemplating a substantial donation to the diocese."

The Bishop looked quickly at his calendar. "Perhaps Tuesday for lunch would be better. Yes, make it Tuesday. You say he's rather indirect in his speech?"

"He hates to say things in so many words, if you know what I mean."

"Yes, I've met men of that type, some of them very fine persons. Well, Tuesday then."

His eyes became vague, darting back and forth across his

desk. It was clearly time to leave. I rose and went over to kiss his ring. He granted his hand, deprecatingly.

"It isn't needful," he said. I turned toward the door.

"Oh, one other minor point, Father. I suggest that you have your suit dry-cleaned before Tuesday. I noticed a spot on your lapel."

He smiled to take the sting out of his remark.

"I'm a stickler on such points, I'm afraid. Don't be offended. A spick and span appearance is very important in these times."

I was somewhat disgruntled as I received my unbrushed fedora from the spick and span maid. Speaking of clichés — what was "spick and span"? The Bishop, I thought, would do well to follow his own advice. However, my depression was easily cast aside. I had been invited to the Bishop's table. This was an achievement which could be boasted of by only a very few untitled clergy in the diocese. Rumors, I knew, would start at once, as soon as the luncheon visit became known. "Roland is going to be made a monsignor," they would say. It might even be true.

Since Mr. Halligan had invited me for an afternoon's cruise on his yacht the following day, I was easily able to convey the Bishop's invitation.

As we stood alone on the poop deck he grew almost rhapsodic in his appreciation. Was it a tear that I detected in the eye corner?

"I have had a few honors in my life, as you may know," he confessed, "but I would be hard put to evaluate any of them above this latest. To be invited to lunch at the Bishop's table! Surely worthiness cannot be a qualification on my part; rather I am tempted to feel all the more guilty for imposing on the attention of so great a man of God."

He put his hand on my shoulder and looked at me with shining sincerity. "What you have done to foster this will not soon be forgotten in the Halligan household."

He paused a moment to shake off the emotion, like a dog shaking off the remains of a bath.

"Tuesday at one, you say? I just know I have a half-dozen things lined up around that time, but you may believe me, Father, when I say that secondary concerns will not be allowed to impinge on the beautiful moment that has been allotted to me. Primary matters demand primary consideration."

"You mean you'll be there on Tuesday at one?"

"Unquestionably."

I walked down the steps to the main deck and then into the lounge where an aproned sailor was making drinks behind a chromium bar. There were a scattering of slacks- and shorts-clad people sitting in little groups in the large room. One or two nodded my way but from the high tone of the voices it was evident that most of them had had enough drink to be rather oblivious. I had two quick ryes with soda and then went out to the shady side of the deck and lowered myself into a brightly striped deck chair. As the cruise was to be a brief one we were staying close to the coast line. I could see the white cottages on the shore and the brown-skinned bathers on the brilliant beach. Occasionally a motorboat full of youngsters would splash by noisily, with much waving on both sides. I loosened my Roman collar and closed my eyes. The two ryes had made me a little dizzier than I had expected.

"Aren't you Father Roland from the Cathedral?"

I looked up into the bloodshot eyes of a full-bodied blonde who was teetering slightly in the breeze.

"Yes, I am." I tried to put gaiety into my tone.

She collapsed clumsily on the next chair, spilling half her drink in the process.

"Father, I have something I want to ask you. I hope you won't take offense."

"Of course not."

"Sure?" She smiled sillily.

136

"Positive."

"Well, this friend of mine is divorced. Father, why can't she marry again, since she's found a nice man with plenty of money who's dying to make her happy?"

Despairingly, I asked the usual questions and gave the usual reasons. Naturally, the blonde lady, who was practically leaning on me by this time, was not completely satisfied. It was clear that she wanted her nice friend to marry the rich man.

I escaped finally when a compassionate young man in shorts invited me to play shuffleboard. I was a little disconcerted when, during the second round, my handsome opponent said,

"I hope you don't mind my mentioning it, but I have a college friend who's gotten involved in a bum marriage. Now could you tell me . . ."

And so it went, on and off all afternoon. I could only conclude that Mr. Halligan's friends' friends were the most unhappily married people in the world.

In any case, I was glad to return that evening to the celibate simplicity of the Cathedral rectory. I was painfully sunburned, stomachically queasy, and excessively weary, but I was satisfied that I had courageously carried out the obligations of the apostolate of the rich.

On the following Tuesday when I arrived at ten to one at the Bishop's house, I found Mr. Halligan pacing the parlor moodily. Having cleared his desk and canceled untold appointments to be present on this occasion, he no doubt had expected to be received in immediate audience. He gave me a curt acknowledgment and continued his pacing. I felt almost as though he had lost interest in me now that he had entered the Bishop's house. He said nothing and took no notice as I examined the bric-a-brac on the marble mantelpiece.

At precisely one by the mantel clock there were footsteps in the hall and Monsignor Semple hurried into the parlor, with the Bishop close behind. His Excellency was most gracious in his reception of my friend. Smiling, he deprecated Mr. Halligan's feeble knee bob and snatched his ringed hand quickly from the eager Halligan lips. My introductions, carefully rehearsed, were all but lost in the commotion. It seemed that two kindred spirits had taken warmly to one another at first sight. Even Monsignor Semple was smiling. Although ignored, I felt a glow of accomplishment. I had been responsible for bringing about a meeting of moment.

"Your Excellency," panted Mr. Halligan, "my dear wife, had she been able to be present — she is ill, you know — would have considered this one of the proudest moments of her life. I confess that I would have had to endorse her point of view."

"Tut, tut. I am so sorry about Mrs. Halligan. But Father Roland, I understand, has been taking excellent spiritual care of her."

They both looked at me appreciatively. Proud to be acknowledged, I looked happily down at a cornucopia pattern in the Turkish carpet. I thought that perhaps, after all, I might play a larger part in the luncheon than I had anticipated. But in this I was mistaken.

After a few more moments' conversation about Mrs. Halligan's illness, His Excellency led us into a richly ornamented dining room, a splendid example of rococo decoration.

"Lovely," Mr. Halligan murmured as he was directed to the seat of honor at the Bishop's right.

It was a conversation piece, the room, and it carried us successfully through the soup course. The Bishop was on familiar ground and proffered a number of witty anecdotes about the hangings and the furnishings, with a reference here and there to his predecessors' problems in putting to effective use the various art objects of which they were frequently the recipients.

By the time the spick and span waitress had served the

roast turkey, they had discovered many mutual friends. Here the conversation became extremely animated and exclusive. Apart from an occasional episcopal glance in my direction, I was ignored. Monsignor Semple, more experienced, interjected an occasional grunt, or laugh of appreciation, and once or twice supplied the Bishop with an interesting fact.

At the cherries jubilee, I sensed a certain tension settling over the table. The luncheon was nearly over and nothing positive had been accomplished. Monsignor Semple's normally worried frown became somewhat deeper. The Bishop, although bland as ever, seemed a trifle distracted and some of his bon mots were a little carelessly shaped. My heartbeat quickened. Suppose that I had brought in a free-loader, seeking personal prestige at the expense of the Bishop's luncheon table. I felt panicky.

Now there was a complete silence except for the squish of teeth against cherries. But then, Mr. Halligan cleared his throat and I could sense immediately that the day was saved.

"Your Excellency," he said portentously, "I have the good fortune to possess a large estate just twenty miles from the city. My wife has often said that it would make an ideal convent school for girls. We would be privileged, if . . ."

I went back to the rectory joyfully. I had been the means of providing a new school for the diocese. My apostolic zeal had been well rewarded. I would not soon forget the Bishop's smile and warm handclasp — so full of promise — as I bowed my way out of his residence. . . .

But my success was brief. The deed was not delivered to the diocese quickly enough and Mr. Halligan's subsequent indictment for stock fraud brought with it a lien on all his property. Halligan Hall never came into the possession of the Bishop.

Perhaps it was just as well. In any case, the Bishop was most gracious about the disappointment. He has never held it against me.

CHAPTER IX

WHEN the Bishop appointed me as an assistant in the Diocesan School Office, my friends congratulated me enthusiastically and predicted that the monsignorial "purple" was only a matter of months or at most a year away. This hardly consoled me because I doubted if papal honors would ever be my lot and because the anticipation of sitting in a desk chair for the bulk of my priestly life was not reassuring.

However, I had "made it," as my friends put the matter, and possibly I would discover that office work had its fascination even for a priest. In point of fact, I was to find that school administration problems were sufficiently interesting and varied to make my job something of an adventurous experience. It was only the routine of correspondence, reports, and commonplace interviews that made me feel at times like going for a long country walk. I must say that I developed in this time a great pity for stenographers, clerks, and bookkeepers. These are the hidden martyrs of our age. To spend a lifetime or even several years in such work seems to me to require patience and fortitude in a heroic degree. It would be difficult to invent more dehumanizing work than that which is the daily lot of these unfortunate people.

My own work had many interesting moments. The "Our Father" controversy was one of these.

It started calmly enough. Several Protestant ministers wrote a joint letter to the leading daily urging the recital of the Lord's Prayer by the students in public schools at the beginning of class in the morning. In the letter, they pointed out — rather naïvely — that there was nothing "sectarian" or divisive about the Our Father and there was no reason why it could not be sincerely uttered by any believer in God. Atheists among the children could of course abstain from joining in the prayer if they wished.

The newspaper backed the ministers' proposal editorially and called upon the Mayor to take appropriate action. The Mayor, whose policy was normally to avoid involvement in everything possible, was embarrassed into appointing a committee to investigate the feasibility of the suggestion and to frame, if desirable, a proposal for official action. Needless to say, a member of the Catholic School Office was requested to sit on the committee. Monsignor Bosch, the chief, asked me to "carry the ball," as he put it. His idea of a perfect assistant was one who, without urging, would "pick up the ball and run with it."

When he leaned his lumpy frame over my desk and I felt his breath on my face, I knew I was to be designated for a job of work.

"Don't go out on a limb," he told me as he gently deposited the Mayor's letter on my desk. "The worst thing in these matters is to commit yourself to an extreme position. Stand by principle, of course, but don't be overaggressive. This is the age of suavity, you know that. Your Cathedral training won't hurt you there. Make your point but ram it home with a velvet glove. You know. Some of these ministers and rabbis are pretty slick; before you know it they'll maneuver you into a public position which they will then proceed to describe as another example of the 'inflexibly undemocratic attitude of the authoritarian Church.' I know; I've been caught with my 'authoritarianism' showing. The papers love to print that sort of thing; they particularly enjoy a squabble among 'ministers of religion.' And, of course, watch out for the atheists. I'm sure the Mayor has put a professional free-thinker or two on his committee. This is considered fair play. You know. Well, watch your moves carefully. If you need me, let me know."

He nodded and began to move away from my desk.

I said, "Hold it, Jeff." He liked to be called Jeff.

"Did I forget something?"

"You certainly did."

He shook his strange elongated head.

"What did I forget?"

"What is our policy on this matter? Where do we stand? Theologically it's rather ticklish."

He nodded sympathetically. "You've got a problem. I thought you knew our policy on these things. We favor the general idea of introducing a greater recognition of the Deity and of moral values into the public schools, but each proposal has to be judged on its own merits. We don't want our children forced to attend Protestant services or to listen to readings from the King James Version. You know all this. For the children in a class to say a simple nonheretical prayer together is fine."

"Don't forget there's a Catholic and a Protestant version of the Lord's Prayer."

He suppressed a yawn. "That's always a problem. Maybe each student could say his own version. Or perhaps the committee will come up with some alternate prayer with words agreeable to everyone. Just keep alert and don't let them compromise you on any essential point. But don't be belligerent."

He studied my mild countenance for a moment.

"I don't think you'll provoke any fights."

But Monsignor Bosch had underestimated me, or at least the explosive nature of the situation.

When I arrived for the first meeting at the ugly Education Building several reporters and photographers were there.

The flash bulbs blinded me. For a moment I stood uncertainly.

"What's your name, Monsignor?" a rummy-faced reporter called.

Other questions followed: What was the Catholic position on this matter? Would we object to Catholic students' being led in prayer by non-Catholic teachers? Would we insist on the Catholic version of whatever prayer was decided on?

I fended them off. I said I would prefer not to make any statements until the committee had a chance to meet. I learned later that some of the other committeemen were not so restrained, no doubt working on the principle that he who strikes first strikes best. The freethinker, Gilhooley, made several belligerent statements and had a belligerent picture in the evening papers. I received brief mention as "Diocesan Director of Catholic Schools," a promotion which I hoped would not have any unhappy effect on Monsignor Bosch's ulcer.

I hope that I am not prejudiced but I have rarely been in a community-owned building which did not depress me by its nondescript furniture and its general air of unkemptness. The Education Building was true to civic tradition; the board room with the long green-covered table reeked of unchanged air. Its floor was scuffed and unpolished, the rug was threadbare, and none of the chairs matched. Already the scarcity of ash trays was causing one weasel-faced committee member to dump his ashes on top of a piece of cardboard. The battered carafe with four smudged glasses completed the unpretty picture. Fighting off the desire to turn about, I walked over to the bespectacled gentleman radiating good will at the head of the table.

"I'm Father Roland, Catholic School Board."

"Delighted to have you, Father. I'm Winston McTagg, the Mayor's representative. I'll be acting as a sort of chairman, or perhaps referee if there are any foul blows."

He laughed dryly, thinly, his frightening unrimmed glasses sparkling in the raw light.

I tried an appreciative grunt. "Good stuff," I said inanely. "Good stuff."

"I've always had a great admiration for your Pope. And of course I have many fine Catholic friends."

The usual appalling condescension. I moved away toward a ring of divines at the other end of the table. They nodded to me cordially and we introduced ourselves. I discovered that there were both ministers and rabbis in the group. One of the ministers, a desperately tall and thin man, muttered to me between clenched teeth,

"Look in the corner there and you'll see as nice a pair of freethinkers as you'll ever want."

I looked toward two stout gentlemen engaged in animated discourse.

"They'll blow this thing sky-high if they can," he continued, leaning toward me confidentially. "Also I don't trust one of those rabbis. He's a so-called liberal, very far to the Left. I've had dealings with him before in the matter of released-time instruction. And of course, Hopkinson, the Unitarian — he's standing two to my right — will sabotage the whole program if he has a chance, and grab all the headlines in the process. He's made a career of objecting to everything we try to do. Watch out for him."

My informant's voice was a little louder than he realized and I was hoping that Dr. Hopkinson had not overheard the uncomplimentary description. But he was smiling vaguely in the direction of the liberal rabbi, and his small, dumpy appearance made him appear anything but formidable.

My thin friend, the Episcopalian representative, now strode

up to the beaming McTagg, who nodded agreeably and then proceeded to rap the side of the table with a ruler. Soon we were all in position in our nondescript chairs and the meeting began — without a prayer.

McTagg was obviously going to play a cagey game. His choice of words and his tone of voice seemed to convey an equal indifference toward either the adoption or rejection of the prayer proposal. He took pains to emphasize that the Mayor, whom he represented, was a sincerely religious man but that His Honor would not want to make a decision which could in any way violate anyone's constitutional rights and had hence called upon us to present a recommendation which would be acceptable to all — an obvious impossibility, it seemed to me. Looking at Gilhooley and the other free-thinker, plus the liberal Rabbi and the obstructionist Unitarian, I had a definite presentiment that the problem would eventually end in the courts. I was even more convinced of this when I heard them talk.

Gilhooley, a crude belligerence lurking beneath his fat suavity, grew eloquent about the "traditional American doctrine of separation of Church and State," a doctrine which he naturally indicated could be interpreted in only one way — his way. The liberal Rabbi and the obstructionist minister seconded Gilhooley's sentiments, with pious stress however on the importance of religious training in the home. The Reverend Hopkinson annoyed me slightly when he referred to "our concept of religious freedom unlike that of certain authoritarian churches," and looked significantly in my direction. In fact all the speakers seemed to direct their remarks toward me, as though I had been the prime mover behind the present deliberations.

Hopkinson finally became offensive and I had to intervene. He used the occasion to bring in the Galileo condemnation, the St. Bartholomew Massacre, Fox's *Book of Martyrs*, and Franco Spain.

"All these," he said movingly, "are examples of the way in which some religious groups of authoritarian character attempt to impose their religious beliefs on others."

I was on my feet immediately, just a little angry, but still able to remember Monsignor Bosch's admonitions.

"Mr. McTagg," I said, "I must protest these thinly veiled insults to the Church I represent. I must say that I was surprised that Dr. Hopkinson forgot to include Guy Fawkes in his bill of particulars. These half-true historical clichés have, I think, become nauseating even to many non-Catholics by reason of their unending repetition if not of their inaccuracy. Apart from that, I cannot see what bearing all this has on the problem before us. If Dr. Hopkinson wishes to attack the Catholic Church, may I respectfully request that he make use of his own pulpit and not impose his views on this committee, which has a well-defined job of work to do."

The Episcopalian nodded delightedly toward me when I sat down. The conservative Rabbi looked with interest in my direction. I was pleased with myself. That ending had been good, and there had been a touch of amused irony all through my remarks — just the sort of thing for a situation like this. Dr. Hopkinson's face was red, but he said nothing more for the rest of the meeting.

The Episcopalian, Dr. Rutgers, pressed very hard for the Lord's Prayer at the beginning of every public school day. He noted the several references to the Deity in the Declaration of Independence and the traditional American spirit of reverence for God, and could not see "why any God-fearing human being could object to prayer to God in school or out." He referred sadly to the irreverent tendencies of modern youth and the growing enthronement of secularist attitudes in schools and colleges. This proposal, he said, would help, in some degree, to correct these evils. He spoke with great sincerity in a loud, cracking voice and he accompanied his remarks with sweeping gestures. It was clear that he was the local founder of the "prayer-in-school" movement.

Gilhooley had been squirming during Dr. Rutgers' remarks and, at their conclusion, he immediately signaled for the floor.

McTagg, still beaming through his bright glasses, ignored him and recognized a conservative Rabbi.

This man's views were new to me at the time and I found them surprising. He stood stolidly in his black suit and spoke with an almost overwhelming gravity in a sonorously sepulchral voice.

"The position of those whom I represent in this matter of introducing religion into the public schools is clear," he said. "We are opposed to it. We are ready to grant everything that Dr. Rutgers has said, but we still maintain that the home and the synagogue or church are the places for religious activities and instructions. We have found, by sad experience, that when religion is introduced into educational institutions of a public nature, it always has a Christian coloring which, in turn, tends to heighten the differences between Christians and Jews; and we are always the ones to suffer from such an emphasis. To be very frank, we prefer not to have religious matters raised at all in public circumstances because we have found that prejudices which lie just below the surface of students' consciousness are then brought out into the open. It is better not to bring up the question of religion in public schools if doing so will create divisiveness and ill will."

He spoke at some length on these lines — very frankly, I thought, and perhaps with some basis in history. When he went on to emphasize that the Lord's Prayer was a Christian prayer, I knew that we were going to have to find a substitute, perhaps write one of our own.

Gilhooley, when he finally gained the floor, let loose a bellowing attack on the efforts of "organized religious lobbies to impose their way of thinking on the free children of free American parents."

It was Dr. Hopkinson's attack on Catholics applied to all organized religion.

"It may surprise you gentlemen to know that I do not believe in God and that I have trained my children in the same way of thinking. In so doing I am exercising my rights under the American Constitution. There are thousands, millions more like me. What about the rights of our children not to say prayers in school? I know what you'll say. You'll say they don't have to say the prayers if they don't care to pray. But what happens? These children are made scapegoats of the others, singled out for contempt and ridicule, certainly embarrassment, for refusing to compromise with their beliefs. A harmful divisiveness is thus established and a nonbelieving child is forced into a religious orientation. It won't do, I tell you."

His voice became louder.

"I'm giving you fair warning, one and all, that my associates and I will take this proposal, if it's adopted, to the highest court in the land, if need be, and then beat it to the ground. We will never allow religious lobbyists to stamp out freedom of thought in the 'land of the free and the home of the brave!' "

With a flourish of his cold cigar he sat down to the applause of his companion. The conservative Rabbi looked half approvingly in his direction. He was happy, I suppose, to find someone who agreed with him on the divisiveness of prayer.

It was my turn now to read a statement which I had scribbled that morning in the office.

"The Catholic Diocese," I read, "encourages any reasonable steps which will assist the implantation of spiritual values in public education. Certainly to begin the school day with prayer for God's guidance and blessing is a minimal move in the right direction. Although Catholics are not permitted, by the nature of their faith, to engage in non-Catholic religious worship, we believe that the utterance of a nonsectarian prayer by a group of school children in a classroom would not violate Catholic principles in the matter, and would, in fact, be something of real spiritual value. We deplore any suggestion that such a procedure would cause divisiveness but rather feel that students who pray together will play together and work together in greater harmony. At the same time we reserve our right to approve or disapprove of whatever prayer may be chosen and to withdraw if this program should assume a sectarian coloration."

I sat down amid nods of restrained approval. Even Gilhooley looked pleasantly in my direction.

The remaining speakers gave varying degrees of endorsement to the prayer proposal and when McTagg called for a vote on the proposition, it was approved by a slight margin. The approved motion did not specify what prayer was to be said.

Gilhooley's voice crackled across the room. "Since people are reserving rights here, I and my fellow negatives reserve our right to submit a minority report to the Mayor."

McTagg nodded generously. "Granted, of course. I know the Mayor will be happy to study your views."

"He'll be sorry he ever got into this thing," Gilhooley muttered — happily, I thought. No doubt he relished the possibilities for publicity and oratory which a fight of this type would offer him. He would have been a disconsolate man if his side had won the vote.

After McTagg had appointed the liberal rabbi, Dr. Rutgers, and me to a committee to recommend suitable prayers, we adjourned until the following week. There were still several battles to be fought.

It was raining when I left the unsavory building, a fine, penetrating rain that immediately erased the crease in my trousers. I hailed a cab and slumped listlessly in the back. I felt depressed, a phenomenon which I later noted to be a characteristic effect of meetings and groupings of the type I have described.

As I looked miserably out at the gloomy day, I wondered if Gilhooley's bloc did not stand to gain more than did the spiritual forces of the community. I could picture endless rows of school children monotonously chanting a prayer which, by reason of routine, had become meaningless to them, and all the while Gilhooley and his cohorts gaining publicity in courtrooms and coliseums with virulent and penetrating attacks on the freedom-destroying qualities of the "lobbies of organized religion."

Clearly no one would be completely happy with whatever our committee produced, but as I paid the cab driver I told myself that I had struck a blow for God today, and that monotonous acknowledgment of a Supreme Being was infinitely better than none at all. By the time I reached my cubbyhole office, my bounciness had returned.

Monsignor Bosch was out at another committee meeting of some kind, and I was able to spend the rest of the working day dictating regretful letters to mothers and fathers who had appealed to our office for assistance in enrolling their children in Catholic schools. Sally, a fat, redheaded stenographer, gum-chewed her way through most of these until finally I looked up and saw tears rolling down her freckled cheeks. Then she sobbed openly. It seemed I was giving her too much to do, and she was so tired. I released her and she sent in Rosie, who looked like her twin sister and who also seemed to like gum.

At last the work was done and I picked up my hat. As I snapped off my light, the receptionist rang my phone buzzer.

"There's a man here to see you," she whispered. "He looks and talks like a nut — very loud, very crazy. Shall I get rid of him?"

"I'll see him."

I walked into the outer office and saw the "other" freethinker, Gilhooley's associate, who had been absolutely quiet and calm at the meeting. Now it was clear either that he had been drinking rather heavily or that he was having a mental seizure of some kind. Wild-eyed, his hair pointing in four directions, the chubby little man ran up to me and began to wave his finger under my nose.

"You pawn of the Roman Church!" he screamed. "You and your bosses would take over this country in a minute if we let you. Force prayers down the throats of our children, will you? You'll find your own throats in a noose if you aren't careful."

"Easy," I said sweetly. "You're exciting yourself."

The girls from the other office had come in. They were openmouthed, in shock.

"I heard what you said at the meeting," he shrilled. "I was dying to reply only I promised Gilhooley that I'd keep my mouth shut. But now I'm going to tell you something, Mr. Priest!"

He was pressing almost against me now. I could not smell alcohol. I did not take my eyes off him, but I could see Rosie easing out of the room toward what I hoped was a telephone.

"You people don't allow religious liberty and yet you demand it for yourselves. Look at Spain! What a disgrace!"

I said: "Look at Ireland, France, Belgium, etc., etc."

I moved back a step. His finger had just brushed my nose.

"Nonsense. You say you don't want to bring the Pope over here, but I know better. I've got documents here that will show what liars you are."

He fumbled in his pocket and pulled out a copy of a "hate sheet" which I recognized immediately.

"Your documents are not very reliable."

"What?" he shouted. "You, you rotten black crow of a

tool of Fascism, you dare to question my documentation? Why, I'll carve the truth on your yellow belly."

At this point he pulled out the knife, a switch blade of ugly proportions. One of the girls screamed and another rushed forward.

"Stay where you are, girls!" I said in a low-pitched tone. "Our friend is just excited. I'm sure he doesn't mean any harm. Do you, my friend?"

At this he let out a war whoop and rushed at me.

Even a rat at bay will fight; I was not experienced at this sort of thing but my reactions were quick and even effective. I grabbed the knife-wielding arm with both hands and twisted it until he dropped the weapon. He punched my face with his free arm and then embraced me in a bear hug and began to kick my shins. In a moment we were rolling on the floor to the tune of curses and imprecations which he released in an unremitting stream. This annoyed me more than anything else, I felt he should have been more restrained in the presence of ladies, one of whom was dancing around us, attempting, unsuccessfully, to bean him with a large telephone book.

But weight and youth will triumph in the long run. I had my mad freethinker pretty well subdued by the time the police and, unfortunately, the reporters arrived. As my opponent was dragged away I ruefully surveyed the shambly office. Monsignor Bosch, on his return, would be disappointed with the appearance of things.

The reporters got very little from me except my name, but that was enough. The morning papers had a full story of the committee meeting and of the battle afterward. I do not think that the freethinkers' cause was helped by the insanity report on Gilhooley's side-kick, but no doubt they had thoughts of picketing the psychiatric ward and claiming false imprisonment. In any case Gilhooley appeared alone at the next committee meeting.

He was obviously ready to fight for the life of his organization, which had been dealt a seeming deathblow by the knife-wielding charter member. His hardening jaw and his braced shoulders promised committee trouble aplenty.

I was bored with it all. In fact, I was beginning to think that life on the school board was not all that I had expected it to be. Great areas of time were frittered away on routine office procedure without much apparent impact on souls and the remaining time was taken up by meetings such as this one, meetings which all too often, it seemed, ended in a frustrating stalemate.

Dr. Rutgers in his opening remarks made it clear that he regarded me as a hero and all freethinkers as villains. This gave Gilhooley a chance to rise to his feet angrily to denounce the provocative actions of the religious lobbies and to deplore the biased press treatment of "the recent unfortunate and unnecessary beating of a very sick man."

I did not bother to reply. The universal laughter of the committee — including Dr. Hopkinson — was sufficient response. Gilhooley sat down with flaming cheeks.

McTagg, conciliatory, unctuous, his rimless glasses sparkling with integrity asked Dr. Rutgers to get on with reading the subcommittee report on recommendations for prayers. Since Rutgers and I had agreed on the phone that the Our Father should be recommended, with the ending optional, the majority report of the subcommittee was simple and without surprises. The other member of the subcommittee, Dr. Kleinman, the allegedly liberal rabbi, had informed us that he would submit a minority report.

"I don't trust him," Rutgers repeated to me. "He'll have some smooth trick up his sleeve. Wait and see."

I waited quite a while — an hour in fact — while Dr. Kleinman reviewed the whole matter of Church and State, the First Amendment, the American way, the history of religious intolerance, and the mind of liberal Jewry on the introduction of religious values into public education. He had the same opinion as had the conservative rabbi that apparently innocuous prayers or actions tended in fact to take on a sectarian tone in the context of the American classroom.

"However, gentlemen," he said, "I do not want to be an obstructionist when the laudable idea of worshiping God is to be encouraged among our children. Although I do feel that the home and the church or synagogue are the suitable milieux for religious training, I would certainly find it hard to vote against the pious effort which has come before this committee."

He spoke slowly and in a highly cultured voice. I could see his Phi Beta Kappa key dangling at his vest.

"I think, gentlemen," he continued in his semi-Oxford accent, "that a compromise would be in order and I think that the prayer which I shall recommend — which is not strictly a prayer at all — should be acceptable to all of us who believe in God and in America. Perhaps even our freethinking friends will see their way clear to accepting it."

Dr. Rutgers grunted incoherently across the table in my direction. I smiled back knowingly. The eternal compromise which solves nothing. I looked up at the clouds of smoke gathering in the green light shades. The air was stuffy and stale. For a second I felt nauseous at the vision of a lifetime of such committee meetings. Then Dr. Kleinman announced his compromise prayer which was not a prayer.

"I have noticed," he said, "the popularity of certain patriotic songs which invoke God's blessings on our beloved land. These songs are often sung in public places, and are even purveyed through the entertainment media, without creating any apparent divisiveness. I have noticed that Christians and Jews as well as those with no formal religion show no sense of reluctance to sing these songs — which, as I have said, usually invoke the Deity at one point or another. Therefore I am happy to submit to this committee the proposal that

154

every school day should commence with the singing of 'My Country 'Tis of Thee,' as it is popularly called. This song contains a very reverential appeal to the Almighty in a spirit of fervent patriotism."

Immediately there was a murmuring and several hands were raised. McTagg, a nervous smile on his face, recognized Dr. Hopkinson.

With a quick — and snide — glance in my direction, Dr. Hopkinson begged to congratulate Dr. Kleinman on his brilliant suggestion.

"I think," he bellowed sententiously, "that it bordered on a stroke of genius to link a patriotic aspect to the invocation of the Deity. Thus it will be made clear to the children that adherence to a Church should never come in conflict with one's loyalty to his fatherland. Thus the baneful effect of certain authoritarian religions which encourage primary loyalty to foreign states and potentates will receive a salutary countercheck."

Without rising, I shouted, "Would Dr. Hopkinson care to enumerate the authoritarian and unpatriotic religions to which he refers?"

"Certainly, I'll . . ."

But McTagg was banging his gavel and smiling glassily.

"Gentlemen, gentlemen, let's come to order. No recriminations please. I'm sure His Honor would not be happy to hear of bad feeling on the committee."

Hopkinson sat down with obvious reluctance, and several others rose to endorse the Kleinman proposal.

Even Dr. Rutgers was enthusiastic.

"I must confess," he said, "that I have often had occasion to disagree with Rabbi Kleinman in the past on other issues of a religious nature, but, however, reluctantly, I must now praise him for the plan which he has put forward. Naturally — or should I say 'supernaturally' — I should prefer the 'Lord's Prayer' to be selected, but since that is unlikely to

win the wholehearted support of this committee, I am willing
— nay, happy — to cast my vote for what shall be no doubt
known henceforth as the 'Kleinman Proposition.' I would
also like to call your attention to the happy fact that 'My
Country 'Tis of Thee' has the very same air as 'God Save
the King,' a point which cannot help but nourish an even
stronger link between the two great English-speaking
nations."

There were some snorts at this and one or two smiles.

The conservative Rabbi — whose name I never learned —
rose with a sad smile.

"I too," he said sepulchrally, "appreciate my learned confrere's suggestion and admit that it would eliminate most of
the difficulties which have been raised at this table in our
previous meeting. I would, however, call to his attention
and that of the other members a phrase in the song 'My
Country 'Tis of Thee' which is unfortunately divisive in
character. I refer to the words 'our fathers' God' which occur
at one point in the song. This is an apparently innocuous
phrase, my dear friends, but its prejudicial possibilities are
appalling. 'Our fathers' God.' Just think of that for a moment.
Think of all the conflicts and strifes of a religious nature
which it calls to mind. Is this the Protestant God, or the
Catholic God, or the Jewish God? I know you will say that
we all believe in the same God. But the children will not
think merely of this. The presence of the term 'our fathers''
will immediately give a sectarian tone to their thinking, and
since most of their forefathers were Protestant, this will place
Catholic and Jewish children at an immediate disadvantage
giving them a sense of inferiority and perhaps leading to act
of discrimination on the part of the Protestant students. From
such innocent circumstances do religious conflagrations grow
Regretfully, therefore, I must ask that Dr. Kleinman's propo
sition be rejected."

My opportunity had now arrived. I felt that with the

prestige I had recently gained as a result of the mad free-thinker's attack, I could win almost unanimous support for an idea which had just popped into my head.

"Mr. McTagg and gentlemen," I burbled, "may I suggest that our school children begin the day by singing the song 'God Bless America'? Certainly to this there can be no objection. It is a relatively new and popular song; it refers to God and also to our country. It does not allude to 'our fathers' God,' and it has an inspiring lilt."

As I had hoped, "God Bless America" won the day — almost unanimously. Gilhooley had been strangely silent since Dr. Kleinman's proposal, and when the vote was taken he simply remarked, "Not voting," with a strange leer.

McTagg ran immediately to the phone and obtained His Honor's wholehearted endorsement. The members of the press were called in and given the story at once. Committee members pressed around me with congratulations.

Happily I returned to the office to report to Monsignor Bosch.

Sitting back in his chair, he heard my story silently. At last he shook his head and said one word: "Booby-trapped."

"Booby-trapped? What do you mean? It was the best thing that could be done. I emerged as the hero. What more could you want?"

"Father Roland, for your information every public school class in the city already begins the day by singing 'God Bless America.' This has been true for the past five years."

I spent a red-faced afternoon dictating formula letters to Sally, the redhaired stenographer.

CHAPTER X

I SHALL not go into detail about my transition from the School Office to a chaplaincy in the United States Army. It is sufficient to say that the war, horrible as it was, offered an opportunity to many men, clerical and lay, to escape from some situation which had almost reached the limit of tolerability. Although, as I have said, the school job had its interesting and even adventurous aspects, its work, in general, was to my mind, outside the mainstream of the religious ministry. The close contact with people, the direct ministrations to souls in search of spiritual consolation, the catechism classes, the Church societies, the convert instructions, the apostolate to the sick and poor — these and the other characteristic functions of a parish priest which I had envisioned for myself in the seminary and realized in fact through most of my priestly life were almost completely absent from the scheme of things in the school office. The chaplaincy offered an honorable way out of my difficulty, especially since the Bishop issued a letter to his clergy urging as many as possible to apply for his permission to enlist. I applied, was approved, and received His Excellency's accolade for my action. Here then was a chance for direct and effective contact with souls in need as well as an opportunity to perform an important act of patriotism in a time of great national crisis. I donned a first lieutenant's uniform with satisfaction.

Eventually, after a number of experiences which I need not relate, I found myself in Oran, Africa, attached to an infantry regiment scheduled, in due course, to play an important part in the Italian Campaign. I had not yet been under front-line fire and was almost eager to receive the call to such action. There may have been some pride in this. I often thought with horror of returning to my diocese after the war without ever having been in the front lines. To confess this to my priestly colleagues would have involved an embarrassment which I did not relish even in contemplation.

We were marking time in Oran. I was living in a hotel with numerous other officers, sweating out the days and nights, with few duties, trying to pass the time without wasting it completely. My principal amusement was jeep rides around the countryside during the day and bridge games at night with three other chaplains, including a Presbyterian minister who played as though he had invented the game. He was most charitable in pointing out my frequent blunders but on more than one night as I retired I had a guilty feeling that I had failed the one true Church.

We were playing our second rubber of the night in one of the dingy bedrooms of the evil-smelling hotel when my orders arrived by special courier. Anzio had been taken some days previously and our armies were moving swiftly up the Italian boot. I was to join the Thirty-Fourth Division's Sixth Regiment as field chaplain — at once. A plane was leaving in an hour.

My bridge companions congratulated me. They too were restless. The Presbyterian seemed especially sad.

"You'll have to find another student," I said.

He nodded. "It's not that. I was wondering why you're being sent up there ahead of your unit. Father Harper was with the Thirty-Fourth, Sixth. What's happened to him?"

"Battle fatigue, maybe. They get worn out very quickly in that kind of fighting. Or maybe he's wounded."

"Or maybe he's dead," the minister murmured.

I didn't care to think along pessimistic lines. I said good night and packed my bags. I had an almost ecstatic feeling of well-being as the plane left the ground. Oran could rot. I was going to do a man's work, a priest's work in war.

We landed well back of the lines and I was driven in a jeep by an untalkative infantryman to the headquarters of the commanding officer, a Colonel Waters, who assigned me to a billet in the local inn. I was to work at the field hospital which had been set up in a school on the northern rim of the sleepy little Italian town.

"You have a jeep and a driver, Chaplain," the bloated Colonel announced ponderously. "I advise you to stay close to the hospital. That's where you can do the most good. If you go wandering up to the front lines you may get a bellyful like your predecessor."

"Harper's dead?"

The fat man nodded solemnly. "We sent the coffin back a few hours ago. You must have passed him — it — in the air. Keep close to home and you'll probably be all right; this is not a football game up here. Everyone's playing for keeps."

"You mean you're forbidding me to go up ahead even if there's need for me up there?"

His eyelids trembled slightly as he smiled. Then he poured half a glass of what looked like water — but might have been gin — from the carafe on his desk. "Father, I don't forbid chaplains to do anything. I've been in the army too long for that."

For the first time I noticed the West Point ring.

"This is not a monastery or a religious school," he continued, warming to his theme, "where we forbid priests to do this and that. If you want to go up there, it's your own funeral. I'm just talking sense to you. Just use your noggin

160

and you'll be all right. If I can help it I won't have any more dead or broken-down chaplains on my hands. There's a minister over in the hospital who cracked yesterday; he's a mess. He's been up here too long but the damned G.H.Q. wouldn't send up a replacement. You'll see him when you get over there."

He stood up. "If you need anything — really need it — let me know."

I saluted and went to look for my driver and my jeep. A blond boy soldier of about eighteen approached me as excited as I, and told me that my car awaited me.

"What's your name, son?"

"Private Peters, sir. My buddies call me Sandy."

"O.K. Peters," I said gruffly, "drive me to the hospital, and watch that salute hereafter. It was pretty sloppy."

"Yes, sir."

From the kid's knowing smile and proud posture, I had deduced at once that he might be a fresh boy. I decided to check him in the beginning and then maybe I could relax later. My experience as a teacher was not being completely wasted.

"How far is the hospital?"

"Three minutes."

"Don't you say 'sir' to an officer?"

"Yes, sir. Sorry, sir. Father Harper never insisted on it."

I began to like the boy better after that, and I asked him a lot about Harper and found out, as I had suspected, that the older chaplain — he was fifty — had been a very brave man.

"He got it," the boy said, "when he went up there at night, right in no man's land, looking for the dying. Just my luck I wasn't with him the night he got it. I might have saved him."

Sandy uttered a vulgar word.

"Don't use that kind of language in my presence!" I barked. "In fact don't use it at all, get me?"

161

I was hard on him because I knew now that he was a top-flight kid, and I didn't want him to think I knew it.

"In school, I used to bash kids in the face for using dirty language."

He turned his big fresh smile on me and said, "Yes, sir."

I laughed, and we were good friends in three minutes.

When we drew up to the front door of the school hospital, I was surprised at the pleasant, peaceful atmosphere. There were red flowers in front of the terra-cotta building and a bright green lawn surrounding it. Except for an ambulance in the driveway, there was no evidence of war or war's havoc. One might have thought that children were in the school quietly studying their lessons instead of young men, scarcely more than children, writhing in the agony of fresh wounds. I opened the door and walked into an atmosphere of ether and antiseptic.

Picking up an orderly I moved around the wards, following a routine I had followed many times in many other places — a kind word for everyone, regardless of religion, a whispered absolution for the Catholic men, plus an anointing for those whose chart was marked critical. In the morning I would bring Holy Communion to the patients capable of receiving. Of course some of the men needed a little persuading to make their confession but the difficulties were never too great. In all the war, I recall only three or four soldiers who refused the Sacraments, and I suspect that all of these were mentally unbalanced at the time.

I came at last to the battle-fatigued minister, set off in a little alcove by himself. He lay stiff on the cot, staring at the ceiling, his face pallid, his eyes wide and empty.

"Getting a little rest at last?"

His eyelids did not even flicker. He continued to stare.

I shook his shoulder, not too gently.

"Don't you know a fellow chaplain when you see one? Are you on retreat?"

I laughed; this was a funny thing for a priest to say to a minister. He simply turned his head and vacant eyes toward me and said nothing. I noticed that he was dribbling slightly.

It was as sad a case of battle fatigue as I have ever seen. It gave me a graphic warning of what could happen even to a well-balanced man if he were left too long "up front." I made up my mind to insist on regular relief.

I need not describe some of the bloody sights that I saw, men disemboweled and crazy with pain, waiting, praying to die until dulled once more with the sometimes tardy drugs. The medical problem here was simple: to try to keep them numb until they died.

I was tired when Sandy drove me to the little inn where I was to stay. Even the antics of the landlord, who was a typical moving-picture Italian, did not amuse me. I was more taken by the cool bottle of Frascati which he delivered with a flourish to my broad-windowed room.

"I have just a few bottles, Signor Captain. The Nazis drank most of my wine, but I managed to hide just a little. My wife says always be good to the chaplains, and the Lord will forgive me my sins. But I have not many sins, Signor; I am too old to have sins."

"When was your last confession?"

The old man ceased gesticulating for a moment to give this question the proper amount of thought. At last he shook his head sadly.

"Ah, Padre mio, I am very bad. My last confession was forty years ago when I was married. But I have no sins, Signor Captain, I am too old to sin."

He backed quickly out of the room before I could find fault with his logic. However, I felt sure I could catch him in my net before I moved out. It was just a question of trapping him at the right time. My hospital successes had given me great confidence.

After only moderate success in bathing myself in a hip

bath, I lay down on the huge bed and closed my eyes. The last time I had slept I had been in Africa, and I felt the fatigue crawl up my legs as I stretched out.

Then the enemy planes started to whistle over the town and my sleep was ended. Every time I would doze, another explosion would rock me out of my slumber. Some of the bombs seemed to be falling very close to the inn. Then I realized that I should go down to the bomb shelter to await the end of the raid, and prepare myself to rush to the hospital. New cases would certainly be brought in. Now I could hear the roar of artillery fire, then shortly the sound of more planes, presumably ours, and suddenly the raid was over. Sandy was knocking at my door.

"There'll be some casualties at the hospital, sir."

I pulled on my clothes quickly; my weariness seemed to have vanished and I was eager to be of service. On the way to the hospital, the boy said:

"It's well to get to a shelter, sir, when the bombs are falling. You've never been near the front before, have you?"

"Keep your eyes on the road. It would be well for you to remember that privates aren't entitled to ask officers personal questions. Haven't you learned that yet?"

"Yes, sir. Very good, sir. Father Harper never made a point of it."

I could sense the mischief glinting in his eyes, but I would not rise to the bait. I was silent until we arrived at the flare-lit hospital. This time it was clear that there was a war on. Ambulances were sirening up the path. The air was filled with shouts as sweating stretcher-bearers carried the raid victims into the main corridor. I was busy all night and part of the next morning. The scene was one of such horror that sometimes I still dream of it when I am tired and upset. I have had other even bloodier experiences but the combination of circumstances — my fatigue, Harper's death, the terrifying bombing, and the quiet ride to the hospital filled with screaming victims — seems to have stamped this night indelibly on my subconscious.

At eight o'clock I said Mass on a portable altar and distributed Holy Communion to those capable of receiving. These were not too many. Shock and loss of blood are not good preparations for admitting food — even Divine Food — into the stomach.

At nine I returned to the inn for some breakfast and a renewed assault on the bed. I had two hours' sleep before I was called again to the hospital.

So it went for ten days. I understood then the staring eyes of the battle-fatigued minister, I, who had never been in the line. Always I was half asleep and yet too tense to relax, worried, disturbed, with a sense of urgency surrounding me like an aura wherever I went. And all the while Sandy kept his fresh gaiety, his well-scrubbed look, and his hair unrumpled. Without knowing it, he had a lot to do with keeping me on balance. As events were to prove, he would have a lot to do with keeping me alive.

On the tenth day, when I saw the tanks and lorries rolling past the inn toward the front, I knew that I was going to face more work than ever in a day or two and more fatigue. I decided on a half day's holiday while I had a chance, taking a lunch with me and hiking away from the town into some pretty hills which had been inviting my presence since the day of my arrival. I told no one but Sandy where I was going; in case of emergency he was to come for me.

I pointed to a little patch of silver on the hillside.

"I'll be there," I said, "with my hero sandwich and my wine, and perhaps a good book if I can find one in this unliterary town."

He lowered his eyes innocently. "There are plenty of books around the area, but you wouldn't like them."

"You can go now."

"Yes, sir."

I followed a dusty trail up into the hills. There were some of our gun emplacements there, I knew, but I hoped to avoid them; I was selfish about my half holiday. A knapsack carried the provisions supplied by the innkeeper and I had succeeded in obtaining a small book of poems by Keats. The day was clear and golden, the foliage bright and fresh in the sherry sunlight. Walking along the path through the lattice of shadows formed by the overhanging trees, I felt almost lighthearted — for the first time since my card games in Oran. Other walks in other woods, long forgotten, came alive in nostalgic remembrance. The tramping tours in the seminary hills, summer vacations in the dazzling Berkshires, week ends which I had spent as a youth at my uncle's lodge far away from the city where I lived — these were pleasantly although vaguely in my consciousness.

I found the silvery spring at last and, resting against a tree, puttered through my volume of Keats, finding some of his lines perfect for this ecstatic natural setting. I did not concentrate on the philosophical weaknesses of his romantic pantheism. It was enough to share the uncritical mood of sunny identification with God's creation. War with its man-made ruptures of the shimmering cloak of earth might never have existed. Only the drab of my uniform, though it blended quietly with the colors of the day, offered a check to the innocence of the mood.

I munched happily on my enormous sandwich, relishing it with a new-found glee, and I gulped almost greedily at the goodly flagon of ruby wine. Too soon the meal was consumed, but the satisfaction of hunger and thirst left in their place a happy languor, easeful, sweetly demanding some moments of repose.

I slept perhaps an hour and awoke with a nervous jerk. Then my Keatian mood revived and I bathed my face and hands, Thoreaulike, in the now not-so-silvery waters. The sound of distant artillery fire invaded my quietude. I was drying my face with my handkerchief when the crackle of twigs announced the arrival of Sandy. He was unhurried, smiling enigmatically.

"There's an all-out attack by our men. I thought you might like to know."

He was too casual for a boy his age. Whom was he imitating, what character in what book or movie?

We hurried silently back the way I had come. My hard-earned peace had now given way to a jerky nervousness that almost brought the consumed sandwich to my lips. Half-way down I remembered that I had left my Keats by the spring. But it was too late to return.

At the hospital I regained composure through activity. There was no time to be nervous with truckloads of dying men. Through eight hours I never stopped confessing, anoint-ing, blessing, praying. The non-Catholics too I helped to die as best I could.

There were many tragic requests. "Send this locket to my girl, Father." "Tell my mother I was thinking of her at the end." "My kid brother is in the next outfit. Help him, Father."

I shall not extend the litany of last requests, which seemed true and right then but now would look sentimental in cold print. Most of the men said nothing but their prayers and died. Many of course lived on for the long struggle with pain. These too I had to help as I could.

Sandy was beside me always, stepping back only for con-fessions. He would lift these men up or hold them down or turn them over, often with a joking remark which, though crude, the G.I.'s appreciated and understood. He left as many as he could with lighted cigarettes trembling in their lips.

The trucks ceased at last to bring their gory loads, and I had some food in the hospital mess. My head was bobbing over my coffee when Sandy, who had been eating in the kitchen, brought me a new challenge.

"The doctors say there are a lot of wounded still up front, way up. Too bad to be moved. A crew of M.D.'s are going up. Do you want to go?"

My head jerked up and my heart began skipping.

"You don't have to, you know. Actually you're supposed to stay here."

I dredged up some sarcasm out of my fatigue and fear. "Maybe you'd like to wear these crosses. Don't instruct me as to what I'm supposed to do. Get the jeep and we'll follow right behind them."

I wondered what book or movie hero I was imitating.

In the jeep he passed me a flask of brandy. *"Fides Achates,"* I thought.

"I know a nurse at the hospital," he snickered. "She's a cutie, and she knows where the booze is kept."

"That's enough of that," I growled, and gulped at the flask.

There were shell holes on the road and in the darkness Sandy needed all his skill to keep us above ground. Frequently trucks loaded with supplies forced us into the foliage at the side of the road. At last, still following the doctors' car, we arrived at a brick farmhouse surrounded by a guard of silent soldiers. Ahead, not far ahead, there was the sound of sporadic machine-gun fire. We could not have been more than half a mile from "the front."

The corpses and the crippled were laid out on the floor of the large kitchen. Automatically, I unscrewed the cap on my tube of Oleum Infirmorum, Oil of the Infirm, and began my spiritual chores. For once my own personality counted for nothing; I was not myself but "the priest," Christ bringing His forgiveness and His grace that is stronger than death to the front lines.

My work didn't take long. These men were either dead or too close to death to talk. I had to do everything briefly, whispering Acts of Contrition, of love into their deafened ears, pressing a crucifix against their cracking lips. Death rattles filled the room like a grisly symphony. Sandy was beside me, as before, but his cigarettes were of no value here. He was pale in the lantern light and his mouth hung half open. Even he could be shaken. Perhaps it was the puzzled, hurt expression of their eyes. What did life mean? What was war all about? Perhaps the questions bothered him as well.

"Come on," I muttered. "A little air won't hurt."

I had known what was coming all along, had feared it, but felt it inevitable, and so I was not surprised when the quiet little Captain waylaid me en route to the car.

"There are some men 'up there,' out in the open under fire. Two are dead as far as we can make out, and the other three are badly ripped up. They can't last. One of them's been praying out loud and calling for a priest. We can't move them out. Even if we could, it would kill them. But one or two men might crawl out and back. It's a lot to ask. I'll go with you if you like."

"No sense both of us getting killed."

Sandy of course volunteered, but the code into which I had been trapped made me reject his offer.

"Show me where it is and I'll crawl out, Captain."

"We'll cover you as best we can."

He led me through a field up a little rise. Sandy stumbled along behind us.

"Flatten out, Father."

"I hear you, Captain."

The groans seemed almost immediately in front of us. To the side I saw a low slung gun with two men lying behind it. I sensed but did not see the presence of many more.

"Straight ahead, Father, about eighty yards. The Germans are eighty yards farther. If you lift your head they'll blow it off."

What should my answer be? A casual laugh? A nonchalant "Nuts!"?

I had been forced into a role and I had not studied the lines. It really was a "role." This was not I. I was watching myself in a melodramatic movie.

I said nothing and began to crawl slowly, flat against the ground, really eating the dirt.

Halfway there my confidence swelled. The Germans had not seen me. Were they asleep?

Then a flare was lobbed over me. I lay absolutely still.

I felt rather comfortable, as though I might easily fall asleep on the dusty ground. I closed my eyes for a moment with a sense of peace which reminded me of my reverie at the spring. When had I gone on my picnic? Was it years before? Surely not the same day, the same eternity.

The flare died. I could hear the hysterical praying ahead of me, but I could not approve. Hysteria could give us Catholics a bad name. We had not been taught to die this way.

I crawled onward. Was it irreverent to think of the words of the Messianic prophecy, "A worm and no man"?

Another flare. The pink brilliance gave a sort of carnival atmosphere to the night. Overconfident, I lifted my head just slightly to see what lay ahead. In the center of the field there seemed to be a slight indentation. Several G.I.'s lay spread-eagled beside it. The fading voice issued from the center in a frenzied hymn, "Jesus, My Lord, My God, My All."

A bullet removed my helmet as though to remind me of the sacredness of the occasion. Quickly I kissed "this earth" — this Italy.

I heard a chorus of whistles over my head and then some small explosions at the far side of the field. The Captain was at his mortars.

The flare burned out and I wriggled the last twenty yards for a long gain through center — a touchdown in fact, but there was no jubilation to surround my triumph, only a shallow pitful of mangled men and a half-crazed youth whose dying face stared up at me from the ground. A dead body was lying across his chest and another across his legs.

His singing had stopped and his huge, half-glazed eyes stared at me through the darkness.

"I am a priest," I said.

He croaked an acknowledgment and then a request. "Father, would you possibly — possibly have time to hear — to hear my confession?"

Would this be tragic irony? After my hard-earned touchdown. I admit I had to choke off a great laugh.

"Go ahead. Confess."

I heard him out — absolved him, anointed him, blessed him. I had no Viaticum, and besides, he could not swallow. He died as I dabbed the oil from his forehead with cotton.

I crawled now from one corpse to another — there must have been six or seven — whispering Acts of Contrition into dead ears, conditionally administering the Last Sacraments. I did not know if they were Catholics or even Christians. Under the circumstances there was no time to investigate. But *Sacramenta propter homines.*

Now there was another flare and a mortar shell dropped a few yards to one side. My Captain had given the Germans ideas. I started to reverse my field; I was now experienced at crawling. New light came to me. I decided to zigzag, but I had to stop dead, not really dead, when mortar shells began to drop around me. It was hard to understand why the Germans should waste so much ammunition on a chaplain. Was it merely target practice, or did they consider this a matter of honor?

I weighed these points with surprising lightheartedness as I lay in the dust. I could appreciate the sense of fatalism which is said to infect men in the front lines. "When your number's up, your number's up." But I had no sense of impending disaster.

I lay there and thought of what I would do when my day's work was done. Certainly I would have a long swig from Sandy's bottle of brandy. Then I would return to "take mine ease in mine inn." The hip bath perhaps. Without a doubt some cold chicken washed down with Chianti. And then a long repose in my freshly sheeted bed. I would insist on fresh sheets. The landlord's daughter had not been too particular in this matter.

I thought of many things in the few minutes I lay there: the spotless rooms in the Cathedral rectory, the semicomic committee meetings in the school office, the first days of my priesthood when zeal ran high and every Mass, every duty had a sort of special glow about it, when my sense of the supernatural had been so strong that I was almost physically aware of Christ in me and beside me and angels watching over me, and Mary looking down lovingly. And then I realized that during this whole present episode I had not once turned my thoughts to the God whom I believed to dwell within me. I prayed wordlessly, but my lightheartedness was gone for I knew poignantly that I was not the priest that I should have been, and it was a bitter thought.

Now I was tempted to stand up and run for the cover which awaited me fifty yards ahead. As a young priest I would have done it, but the prudence of the forties weighted me down. Goals were to be attained only at a slow pace; one had to crawl to victory.

For a moment the shells stopped and I crawled on — but not far. The barrage was renewed. There was a flash behind me and I felt the sharp paining entrance of shell fragments into my leg — into both legs. In a few seconds both limbs were numb. Despite the first sense of pain and shock, I was remarkably calm. I was tempted to laugh. Hysteria? In another minute would I be singing hymns? I tried crawling again but I couldn't manage it. If I had had something to grasp I could have pulled myself forward, but there was only the

172

flat, hard ground. I reached into my breast pocket and pulled out my rosary. I felt fairly comfortable as I muttered the *Aves*, trying not to think of blood loss or the possibility of more mortar shells.

Five minutes later I heard a low cough ahead of me and saw a figure crawling toward me. Of course, it was Sandy. He lay beside me.

"How is it, boss?"

"Not boss — sir or Father!"

"O.K. Is it bad?"

"How do I know? It can't be too bad or I'd be unconscious."

Another shell exploded very near. I admit I jumped badly — if one can jump with numb legs.

Sandy, the boy hero, was grinning. "Not used to the music yet?"

"Did you come out here to keep me company while I bleed to death? Or are you going to give me spiritual consolation? There's no sense in two of us being dismembered."

Despite everything I was still playing the hard role.

He produced his rope, and tied it around my chest under my armpits. Even my determination to play the Spartan could not hold back a couple of short, muffled screams.

"Not much of a rock," he whispered, and I could imagine his adolescent grin. "Now you'll see our rope trick. See you in port."

Uncoiling his rope as he moved, he crawled rapidly out of sight. Almost immediately the mortars went into renewed action. There were flares all over the field. I thought I heard a low groan in the distance; the rope slackened. But as soon as the flares burned out, I could sense movement again.

I was getting a little woozy now. They had better hurry, I thought. Then there was the tightening of the rope and I was being hauled at amazing speed across the field. Helpless, I felt like a bloater at the end of a fishing line. Some people

173

are fated to appear ridiculous even at heroic moments. I remember thinking that my uniform would be shredded and then hoping that I would have the decency to "lapse" into unconsciousness. But no. The trip had cleared my head and I presume that I was more a laughable than a pitiable sight when I arrived in the Captain's woods — though no one laughed.

Everyone, however, was very cheerful about my condition, just as I was beginning to worry seriously. At first I was not sure whether or not I still had legs; but when they rolled me over and laid me on a stretcher, I could see that my limbs were still intact, although my trousers were ripped and bloody. It was only when they put me in the ambulance and closed the door that I fainted.

Actually it was Sandy who lost his legs, or rather his feet. He had just reached the edge of the field when the shell struck.

I asked to have him near me in the hospital and we lay bed by bed talking a lot, and laughing sometimes. He wasn't discouraged really or downhearted. He had been told that they would give him feet like new. It's true that he had grown a little more mature all at once, but the grin kept breaking through.

All men are proud I suppose, and certainly I have more than my share of the most deadly vice, but I was glad to say to Sandy as he lay asleep each night, "You're a better man than I am." Of course, when he was awake, I treated him as a callow adolescent, but I think he knew how I really felt. For Sandy was bright as well as brave.

When he died from unforeseen complications a short time later, I felt as though I had lost a well-loved son. And the pain of loss remained with me for a long, long time.

174

CHAPTER XI

Wʜᴇɴ I left the army, I had not been back in the States even a month when the Bishop appointed me as pastor of St. Thomas Aquinas Parish in Royalton, a small but busy industrial city on the bank of the only seagoing river in our state. Older men than I were still assistants, but the Bishop, I presume, wished to reward me for my war service and for my wounds, which in fact never bothered me greatly except to encourage a slight limp on rainy days and in otherwise humid weather.

In our diocese every priest, from the day of his ordination, looked forward to becoming a pastor. This was considered the earthly crown for one's efforts in the service of God and the Church. From the time a man had attained ten or a dozen years in the priesthood, his conversation would be punctuated as a matter of course with wry allusions to the day when he would be a "boss." Announcements of new pastorates were awaited with an almost breathless interest and many knowledgeable priests were acutely aware of just how many men were "ahead" of them on the list of future parish shepherds. In some cases a tearing tension was built up as the cherished goal was approached. And when an appointment came through, the joy of the lucky individual was a shining and beautiful thing to behold. A glow suffused his face for weeks, perhaps months. I have always thought the state of happiness comparable, in an analogous sense, to that of a bridegroom in the early stages of his marriage to the most lovable girl in the world.

Was this attitude — is this attitude — wrong? Out of line with the detachment which should characterize the priest of God? Does it flow from ambition, self-centeredness, the pride of place and power? I shall not here attempt an essay on this theme, but I will say that I think this desire for a pastorate can and often does derive from justifiable priestly motivation: from the legitimate desire of a priest to exercise the fullest possible influence (short of the bishopric) of his consecrated personality on the world in which he lives, from the urgency inherent in a divinely free human being to attain the full scope of his freedom, from the tendency of both nature and grace always toward a higher degree of both state and function, and negatively from the understandable drive to avoid the heavy burden of frustration entailed by the denial of such basic human needs. Of course denials of this type can and must be borne frequently in the priesthood as in every phase of life, but the virtue involved in patiently accepted frustration does not render the fulfillment of the need any the less desirable or pressing.

Am I rationalizing my own reactions on the occasion of my appointment as pastor? Perhaps. But I must candidly admit that I was overjoyed to receive the Bishop's letter. For some time I had the "glow," as they used to say in the seminary, a state of emotion of which I had thought I was no longer capable. I had only one reservation: that the Bishop might more justly have appointed me to a larger parish in a larger city, but this tiny mote in the eye of my exultation bothered me little. I was my own man at last.

I was soon to relearn that fulfillment in principle and in fact can be as far apart as infancy and old age.

The town and the parish reminded me somewhat of my first assignment, although relationships were on a more impersonal basis. Priests were scarcer now because of the war years; I had only one assistant, a boyish but desperately sincere young man named Bob Greene, who was the idol of the parishioners. Fortunately he liked to work, so that I could depend on him for a great deal, although at times I was disconcerted by his tendency to treat me as an old and sick man. He seemed to take it for granted too that I was ignorant of the latest theological emphases and the current social trends in the Church. But since I had never been too far "away from the books," I think I surprised him more than once, a fact which gave me childish pleasure. I had always tried to "think young"; we had not yet reached the era of "thinking big." At least I had not reached it; my curate was ahead of me in this respect.

"Thirty per cent of the Catholics in this little city don't go to Mass on Sundays," he said to me one evening over the nauseating prune whip which the indefatigable Mrs. Pearse had prepared for us.

I spooned another dose into my mouth before I answered. I have always been irritated by people who announce unpleasant truths at the dinner table, particularly in conjunction with the prune whip.

"How do you know?"

"We took a census six months ago."

He stirred his coffee innocently, his eyes cast down, his crew cut and his rounded adolescent features giving him the appearance of a Yale boy in a choir cassock. Even his voice had a Yale boy tone, with its long vowel sounds and its softened "r's." Gone were the proletarian tones of the prewar clerics.

"I'm shocked to hear it, although I suppose it's a sign of the times. You have ideas, I suppose."

He looked up now, all sincerity. "Yes, Father, I think

developing the Lay Apostolate is the answer. Oh, I know you may not be too friendly to the idea; most older priests don't seem too sympathetic to the plan, at least as far as the United States is concerned. The late pastor would never give me a definite answer. But if you'll just give me a chance to try it out, I'm sure a lot of good can be accomplished."

The pleading note annoyed me even more than the dessert.

"If you'll just give me a chance," I said, "perhaps I may be permitted to say that I am all in favor of the Lay Apostolate and always have been. In fact I've read everything I could find about the Jocist movement in Belgium."

He smiled broadly. "I'm delighted to know that, Father. I can count on your approval then? And perhaps your support?"

"Certainly on my approval. Of course on my support. In fact I may take the plan away from you and run the group myself."

His face tensed for a moment and then relaxed. "I wish you would take charge. The pastor is always more effective than an assistant."

Talk is cheap. I wasn't ready for a big operation after only a month in the parish.

"I don't know the people well enough yet," I said lamely. "But I'll be there when you need me."

Mrs. Pearse, gargantuan, projecting power and superiority, pushed open the swinging door from the kitchen.

"Did you ring?" she rasped.

"No," I said meekly and looked at my watch. She was letting us know that it was time to vacate the rose-papered dining room. As I pushed back my chair, I wondered if I would ever have the courage to put Mrs. Pearse in her place; to quiet her when she seasoned my breakfast with her endless praise of the late pastor, to order her to turn down the kitchen radio during meals, to insist that she throw out all her packages of prune whip and buy no more. At the moment

I was too weak. Nothing in my training had qualified me to deal effectively with dominating housekeepers.

I walked from the room in dignified silence.

I climbed the crackling stairs and found solace in studying the parish account books which lay open upon my carved oaken desk. This again was for me a new experience. My personal finances had always presented a relatively simple although often discouraging problem, but complicated debits and credits in long detailed columns had never confronted me until now. Actually I felt that the keeping of books would not be, in my case, the distasteful task which it seemed to be to some of my newly appointed pastoral colleagues. Figures were definite, clear. They had no emotions to be offended, no arguments to offer, no peculiar ways to be taken into account. They remained quietly in their place, in themselves unchanging, definite, offering no opposition, no problem in psychology. Human beings were another matter. The impact of the housekeeper and the innocent disrespect of the boy priest had left me somewhat disenchanted with human persons, or perhaps, more exactly, with personal relationships. For the moment I was content to pass the time with the loyal unquarrelsomeness of mathematical figures.

As I compared the collections of recent weeks I noticed that each Sunday had brought with it a slight decline in total receipts. The difference was slight — five or ten dollars — but the diminution was relentless. I looked back — or rather in the front of the book. For eight weeks now the total of money received had decreased.

As I stared at the aggressively modern statue of St. Joseph on my desk, I consoled myself with the thought that, despite the downward trend, the parish was still well supplied with funds. Not quite so happily as before, I bent over the ledger for further analysis.

The basket collection, I now noted, was almost the same

from week to week. It was the door money which had dwindled. How could this be? If the door money had dipped, then fewer people were coming to our church. If fewer people were attending Mass, then the basket collection should also have totaled less. For the moment, I was not concerned with the spiritual implications which the figures might contain in terms of parishioners missing Mass or going elsewhere. I was more concerned with the moral implications of the arithmetic with respect to the ushers who collected at the door. It was not necessary to have been long a pastor to reach the probable conclusion that someone had been tapping the till.

I leaned dangerously back in my swivel chair and studied my fingernails. I presume that a canny look appeared on my face, a look which would have been recognized at once by the Baker Street Irregulars. At last I closed the book decisively. I would move slowly but watchfully. . . .

Father Greene was not long in founding his Catholic Action group. In fact I was led to suspect that he had been operating underground during the tenure of the late pastor. There was no other explanation for the well-informed and well-trained group of young men who greeted me at the second official meeting, two weeks later. Some of them I already knew; I noted, with a guilty feeling, that two of them served as ushers at the Sunday Masses.

I do not question young Father Greene's zeal for the apostolate or even his ability to work effectively with the men of the parish, but I must confess that I was somewhat appalled at the almost superficial directness with which he pushed his young apostles into plans and actions.

I had visualized a slow process of development, a gradual flowering of deeply planted thought and spirituality into subtle modes of influence which, in the course of many months or even years, would lead to the beginnings of a Christian renascence in our town. This was clearly not

180

Father Greene's concept. Subtlety and the long-term approach were not contained in his bright lexicon. Already the members were discussing ways to eliminate juvenile delinquency. In fact a thin young man with an evilly pock-marked face and, I suspect, a bad breath, was earnestly outlining steps in a program which would, as far as juvenile delinquency was concerned, make of Royalton the Royal Town which it once had been.

Others joined in the discussion. Father Greene smiled and nodded.

Walker, the pock-marked man, however, was obviously the "leader type." He also happened to be one of our ushers.

The entire discussion centered around his program.

"First," he said, "we have to eliminate the occasions of sin and crime in this city — occasions, which we all know, are provided by adults for the destruction of youth. Delinquent adults give rise to delinquent kids, so let's get at the men in this town who are making a business out of corrupting kids. Other steps can follow. I'm sure that Father Greene has plans for a youth cell. The youngsters can work directly on the young delinquents. We'll work on the adults. Like with like — that's the Catholic Action idea, right, Father?"

Bob Greene nodded benignly. "That's the preferred procedure, Tom."

"Well then, let's get down to cases. What are the corrupting factors supplied by adults to the young people of our town — as if we all didn't know. Let's have some observations. Observe, judge, act — that's the C.A. formula, right, Father?"

"You're talking the right language, Tom."

I felt a little sick. Was Greene actually trying to flatter this strange individual?

Observations were made. The parents were at fault, the schools were at fault, there was a momentary hint, quickly

181

covered up, that the churches were at fault; but more immediately to blame, it seemed, were a bar which sold liquor to teen-agers and two stationery stores which peddled pornographic literature. There was also a dance hall which offered wild music and allowed questionable goings on.

There was general agreement that these establishments would be the first objects of attack.

"When the owners of these places are brought to their senses," Walker said, somewhat pompously, "then we can start in on a more positive program. But the first step in correcting an evil is to eliminate the proximate occasions of that evil. Right, Father?"

"You've got a sound theological basis," Father Greene purred.

Committees were appointed to call on the owners to try to reason them into correcting the obvious abuses. If they refused to co-operate, no threats were to be issued, but a report was to be made at the next meeting. Then further measures could be decided on. In the confusion of voices, I heard the terms "picketing," "ads in the paper," and "announcements from the pulpit."

I began to feel alarmed. The suspicion came to me that some of these men, notably Walker, were out for blood. This particular Catholic Action cell might easily escape my control as pastor, yet I would be ultimately responsible. If things went too far, I could be removed by the Bishop for serious imprudence in the conduct of my office as shepherd of souls. Was I being too squeamish? These men had a definite, practical plan, and certainly the abuses they had described needed correction. But was this the correct way for a Church organization to go about its objectives, so directly, so crudely, so quickly, especially when the dangers of controversy and bad feeling were so great? I rose from my camp chair, although I had originally resolved not to interfere in the meeting.

"Mr. Walker and gentlemen," I said, as casually as I could, "I just have a point of information which I would like to raise."

The room was suddenly silent. Heads turned questioningly in my direction. Father Greene paled noticeably and he sat up stiffly in his chair.

"I was just wondering," I went on in my most pleasant tone, "if this procedure which you have been discussing might not be better left to the police authorities. It seems to me to lie more in their province than in that of a group dedicated to the Lay Apostolate. That's all I wanted to know."

There was a general release of breath and several knowing smiles around the room. Eyes turned encouragingly to Walker, the spokesman. He was kind, almost condescending as he explained to me the errors of my thinking.

"You see, Father Roland," he said, "you have the disadvantage of being new in this little city, and you naturally don't understand yet what we're up against. I don't want to say anything bad against any of the cops. I have some good friends on the force. But the fact of the matter is that the town is wide open, and the authorities never seem to do anything about it. Once in a while, when there are a lot of protests, they'll close some place down, but a month later the owners are open for business as usual. I don't want to blame anyone in particular — that wouldn't be charitable, eh Father? — but the truth is that we're not going to accomplish very much by appealing to the authorities. Am I right, boys?"

There were nods of solemn agreement all around the circle of chairs.

A fat man intoned, "He's right as rain, Father, right as rain," and then settled back with a facial expression of pleased complacency at his sole contribution to the evening's deliberations.

183

I should have blown the whistle — to keep the police context — then and there, but my will was weakened by the fears attendant upon newness in a place and by the uneasy realization that such an action on my part would undoubtedly put an end to Father Greene's — and my — hopes of an effective apostolic cell. Even so I should have done what I thought best; I cannot excuse myself. A pastor has to accept responsibility for the results produced by organizations under his control. Actually I was more to blame for what ultimately happened than was Father Greene. He at least had the excuse of inexperience and even, to some extent, of immaturity. As a man more than twenty years a priest, I could hardly appeal to these deficiencies when the Bishop questioned me later.

I left the meeting that night, however, with what was perhaps an unreasonable suspicion. I was all but convinced that Walker was the thief of the parish funds. His appearance, perhaps, was against him, but more than that, his whole manner, larger than life, sententious, masking what seemed to be a deep-seated contempt for human beings in general, especially for me and even for Father Greene, proclaimed to my uncharitable judgment an individual who would not shy at dirty work of any sort when it suited his convenience. Here, perhaps, my experience and maturity did not fail me in the formation of a decision. I resolved to catch him with his hand in the till.

The following week I was not able to attend the Catholic Action meeting because of a commitment to attend the closing of the Forty Hours' Devotion in a neighboring town. In the succeeding week too I was unavailable for the meeting as the result of a bad cold which kept me in my bed. Father Greene had offered me no information as to the development of the antivice program and I, out of a foolish reluctance to make him feel that I was checking on his conduct as moderator of the group, carefully avoided raising the subject at mealtimes. It was, perhaps, a form of escapism on my part. Subconsciously, I suppose, I did not want to hear what would be distasteful to me. Out of such attitudes disaster can be born.

The first letter arrived on the first day I had fully recovered from my cold. It contained a crude message printed in childish letters on a cheap piece of writing paper.

"Call off your hounds or there'll be plenty of trouble for you and your church."

I showed it to Father Greene at the breakfast table.

He studied it carefully and then nodded with weary sagacity.

"It's in keeping with the mentality of the group we're fighting," he said. "I'm convinced they are only slightly above the moronic level."

"What group?"

He looked at me with surprise. "The organized vice rulers of this city."

"What?"

And then he proceeded to inform me that the campaign had been widened, that pickets had been organized, and that handbills exposing the local corruption had been distributed throughout the city the day previously, when I had been lying peacefully in bed.

I felt a dangerous little prick of anger in the back of my head. "Don't you think you should have consulted me about this?"

Flushing slightly, he looked straight down at his plate. "You put me in charge, Father. You didn't come to the meetings. You didn't ask for information. I didn't want to disturb you when you were sick."

"Well, I think this has got to stop right now. It's way out of line. It's not the province of a church organization to get involved in a thing like this."

"Whose province is it?"

185

"The police department's, the authorities' — it's not our job."

"The authorities do nothing. Walker told you that. In any case, I'm afraid it's too late to back out now."

He handed me the local newspaper which lay on the table beside him. On the front page, under a large headline, was the story of the "Crusade Against Corruption."

For a moment, I regret to say that I hated this slender young man with his crew cut, and his neatly pressed cassock, and his Yale accent.

"Dammit, Greene!" I cried, slapping down the newspaper. "Dammit! This time you've gone too far!"

And picking up my mail, I marched with trembling legs out of the room.

The next morning at about ten o'clock I received a startling telephone call.

"If you don't call off your crusade," a muffled voice said, "you're gonna be sorry, Father. It would be too bad if anything happened to that nice church of yours. Better play safe and lay off."

I called the police station at once and in a few minutes the Chief was in my room, sitting in my easy chair and smoking a cigar. He was a big man, handsome in a way, but with a jutting chin that spoiled the outline of his face. His age, I would say, was about fifty but he still had a bushy crop of black hair.

"We'll put a guard on the church around the clock for a week or so, Father, until you can get Father Greene and his men to come to their senses."

"What do you mean by that?"

He leaned forward and jabbed his cigar in my direction. "Look, Father," he said with a pleasantness that evidently cost him a great effort, "Father Greene is a nice young priest. He wants to do good, make his mark with the people. I can understand that. He wants to organize some men to help the church in its work. All well and good. But he's way out of line on this. Number one, there's no organized vice in the city, and number two, even if there was, it's our job not his to take care of it. If I were you, I'd make him pull in his horns. It's only going to cause a lot of trouble for you and the church, and get the town all upset."

I paused for just a second and then shot my verbal arrow. "If there's no organized crime in this city, why have I received these threats?"

He blinked once or twice and then sat back in the chair and closed his eyes.

"Father, those threats are probably just the work of a crackpot. There are always people who want to get in the act when anything unusual is going on. That's all it is."

"Father Greene and his men seem pretty sure that there's vice on a big scale in Royalton. They're convinced of it."

"Father, they're being carried away by their zeal. I can understand that. I know what they have in mind. There are a couple of bars that occasionally sell drinks to kids and there's a dance hall which caters to a pretty crude type of teen-ager. I tell you, Father, we've had them under observation for some time and as soon as we get sufficient evidence, I promise you we'll move in on them. You have my word on that."

Sincerity resounded in his voice but his eyes were studying his cigar.

"But as for the rest, Father," he continued, "they're living in a dreamworld. There's no organized vice in this town. I ought to know."

"Father Greene's group has no doubt about it."

He leaned toward me again, exuding reasonableness. "O.K., Father, I'll tell you what. If they have any evidence about big-time vice, let them turn it over to me and I'll act on it at once. My word of honor. That's reasonable, isn't it? I have a right, a duty to know, don't I? You know, Father, this whole crusade business doesn't make me or the department look too good in the papers. I resent that a little, Father. That's understandable, isn't it? Why not tell them to give me whatever they have and let me handle it from there on?"

I was tempted. It was the course I would have preferred. I walked over to the side window and looked out at the front of the lovely white Colonial church. An elderly woman was emerging through the center doorway, making the Sign of the Cross again and again. There was no traffic in the street, only the Chief's shiny black car crouching comfortably at the curb. I turned back to the room.

"Why don't you speak directly to Father Greene?" I asked.

He waved his cigar defensively. "You're the boss."

"All right. I'll tell him your proposal. But I'm not going to force him to comply. He'll have to be the judge."

"Sometimes you have to curb young men — for their own good. I have to do it in my department."

I held out my hand. "Good-by, Chief, and thanks for promising me a guard for the church."

"I hope he won't be needed for long."

As he pounded down the stairs, I found it hard to preserve Christian charity in my soul. With a great effort I succeeded in being sorry for him rather than despising him. Then I called Father Greene.

The interview was a re-enactment of the meeting at the morning breakfast table, except that now I was calm, even benign, and I had met and talked to the Chief of Police. Although I could not question that there were factual grounds behind the crusade, emphasis on the virtue of prudence was my strong point.

He paralyzed me with one final sentence. "In view of all the public interest that has developed, it would be more imprudent to stop our efforts now than to continue them."

I turned to my bed for consolation and slept the long and unrefreshing sleep of frustration.

Several days passed without any new developments, at least none which came to my knowledge. I noticed that Father Greene was rarely in for meals and when he was present we both stuck carefully to cheerful topics, I with a heartiness that belied my normal temperament. I gulped my prune whip with apparent relish. I gave no evidence of the fact that Mrs. Pearse annoyed me. Yet I hated myself for hiding underneath protective attitudes and I could not shake the deep feeling that I was not being a good pastor.

One night shortly after the church closed there was a small fire in one of the confessional boxes. The guard saw the flame through a window, rushed into the rectory for a fire extinguisher, and with me as his escort, he succeeded in quenching the blaze before it did more than destroy a curtain and char the wood of the confessional.

"Did you smell anything, Father, when we came in?"

"Smoke . . ."

"Yes, but what kind of smoke? Kerosene, Father, kerosene."

I was trapped more deeply than ever. What move could I make?

The following night, I heard the telephone bell ring and I heard Father Greene's feet on the floor above me as he went to answer the call. I judged I had been in bed two hours; it must have been one o'clock. I followed his progress: the hangers rattling in the closet, the pounding of shoes, the click of the light switch in the hall, the creaking of the stairs, the opening and closing of the front door, the roar of his car as he warmed the motor, and at last the steady droning noise past my front windows, fading at last down the street. It was the usual pattern of the nighttime sick call, mysterious, somewhat frightening, but consoling in a way, especially when someone else was called out.

In less than an hour, he came to me in my room with a burden of trouble too heavy for a young priest, or for any priest.

Clothed in my red bathrobe, blinking my eyes painfully in the light of the naked overhead bulb, I sat crouched in my armchair and listened with sickened heart to his account of the nightmarish trip. Leaning helplessly against the door jamb, he spoke in a colorless voice which trembled slightly at the end of sentences; he sounded like an adolescent boy who had committed a "bad" sin and had at last forced himself to go to confession.

"I was called out on a sick call."

"I heard the phone ringing."

"Yes. It seemed bona fide. A man said that his wife had had a heart attack and that the doctor said she was dying. Could I come? Naturally I agreed. I asked him if she would be able to swallow the Blessed Sacrament. He said she would not. His voice was deep and a little crude in tone. He was not a man of education."

I started to squirm. "What has that got to do with it? What's it all about?"

He ignored my interruption and stared vacantly at the opposite wall.

"He gave me the address, the Benson Hotel on South Street, Room 305."

"I never heard of it."

"It's a cheap hotel. He said he'd meet me in the lobby and escort me up the stairs. There's no elevator. I drove to the hotel and met him in the lobby. There was no one else around, no bellboy, no desk clerk. He was a stocky man, medium height, ordinary looking, a little rough-cut, about forty, very well dressed, and slick. His manner was too bland; I felt a little uneasy, but what could I do? I followed him upstairs. He knocked twice on a door and I heard the movement of feet and then he asked me to enter the room ahead of him. A little worried, I did as he asked. As I stepped into the room the lights went out, the door was slammed behind me, and I felt an arm around my shoulder. Before I knew what had happened there was a blinding flash, and the click of a camera. I ran in the direction of the light, but blinded and in the dark, I could not find the photographer and he ran out the door and slammed it. The woman turned on the light and put on a robe. She was a sort of cheap-looking night-club type, hard. She said, "Father, you'd better call off your crusade," and then she opened the door. There was no one in the hall. I was dazed; I still am. I got in my car and drove around and around for half an hour. I tried to think of something I could do, but there's nothing. I can't go to the police; I can't tell this to anyone but you. What can I do?"

He crumpled into my desk chair and sat staring at the floor, his face pathetically pale under his absurd crew cut.

I stood up, indignant, brave, full of solutions. "We'll go to the Chief right now, swear out a complaint, and insist that he arrest that woman immediately. Then we'll go to the newspaper office and you'll tell them the whole story just as you've told it to me. That's the only way to beat this game. We have to act before they do."

He looked up hopelessly. "I thought of that, but it's no good. The woman has surely cleared out by now, and it's too late to make the morning paper. And if they found out that we'd complained they could have that picture on hand-bills all over town by tomorrow afternoon. And besides, the scandal would be terrible. There'd always be a lot of people who think I got caught and was just trying to cover up. It's no good. What can I do, Father?"

I sat down. "There's only one thing to do if what you say is true. Tomorrow you and I will go down to the Chancery Office and ask to have you transferred to another parish far away from here."

He opened his mouth as though to protest and then closed it tightly. He said nothing. He only nodded his head, nodded his head. . . .

191

My next assistant, Father Rorke, was a little older. He continued the Catholic Action cell, but turned its efforts in a more positive direction. The cell developed an excellent program designed to provide an athletic-social center and study group for the young working men and women of the parish. The abandonment of the old plan was made easier when Father Rorke caught Walker with his hand in the church till.

But the crusade was not a complete failure. At the next election, the administration was turned out, including the Chief, and then the real reform began.

CHAPTER XII

I was appointed pastor of St. Ansgar's Parish in a bon-ton section of the see city a few years later. It was a promotion, my friends said, and it indicated that the Bishop had great confidence in me. I did not argue the point, but it was clear that there was a great deal of burdensome work to be done, in both the physical and spiritual areas. A new rectory had to be built and the people had somehow to be brought more fully into the life of the parish. Attendance at Sunday Mass was good, but apparently no one was interested in Church societies or activities; the parishioners were too occupied in their luxury apartments or in the business and social activities of the metropolis to have time or energy for study clubs, the Lay Apostolate, or liturgical music. This, I was told by my urban peers, was an established fact in a city parish of the higher-income variety. The alienation of the college graduate from the social activities of the parish had begun long before and was not to be corrected now when cultural attractions of a secular variety were so readily available. Moreover, the Catholic schools and especially the Catholic colleges with their all-embracing programs had broken the bond of parish unity long since, and they had educated their products to "look down" on parish priests as men of low culture and dubious learning. Everyone knew that diocesan clergy, by definition, suffered from the grave disability of not being Jesuits or members of any Order, and hence were to be viewed with pity if not with suspicion.

It was in this alleged context that I was to work my points, with the help of two middle-aging assistants who gave me the immediate impression of being terribly tired and of having become long since wistfully resigned to lives of routine sacramental administration and counsel, golf (once a week), and private intellectual pursuits in the secrecy of their own quarters.

Father Mutch, a bald and rotund little man of forty-five, summed up the situation:

"We've tried everything: lectures, choirs, clubs of every type, sodalities, card parties, dances, shows — everything in the book. Nothing works; they won't buy it. There are certain things they want from the parish: Sunday Mass, confession and the other Sacraments, reassuring sermons that are artistic without being too long, and a decent burial. Otherwise, they're not interested. What with city-wide philanthropies and social gatherings in the name of charity, religious order magazines, downtown lectures, and Catholic bookshops all over the place, they don't feel any need of the poor parish priests to supplement their spiritual life. So relax, Father, and do what you can, do what you can, but don't be disappointed if it isn't much."

"But the Bishop says that we've got to build a new rectory. He tells me that this one has been condemned by the Diocesan Building Commission."

Father Mutch took a long look around the room in which we were sitting, the so-called common room, and grunted contemptuously.

"You see those cracks in the wall? They've been there for five years. Do you see those warped floorboards? They were in the same sorry condition when I came here ten years ago. One of these days someone is going to walk too heavily on the staircase and he will end up in the cellar. Don't talk to me about the Building Commission. It's taken them five years to make up their minds to put an end to this clerical firetrap."

I must confess that I joined rather briskly in this ridicule of the Building Commission. It was a favorite scapegoat in the diocese and I am as susceptible as other men to the temptation to belittle. But I could not escape the unfortunate fact that now I was the one who would have to bear the burden of financing and building the new rectory.

My junior assistant, Father Kingsley, a dark man with the absorbed, remote expression of a mystic or a scholar, gave me a bit of practical advice.

"Call 'Ecclesiastical Associates,' " he half-whispered in a croaking voice. "They did a superior job of work for Monsignor Dobbin on the North Side. 'Ecclesiastical' will get you all the money you need, and more."

It would not do to accept the suggestions of an assistant too readily — this is against sound pastoral tradition.

"Thank you," I said. "I'll think about it — give it serious thought."

Father Mutch, coming to my room later, strongly advocated "Fundamental Fund-Raisers." It seemed that they had surpassed by 20 per cent the goal in St. Mary's, of which his dear friend, Father Foster, was the pastor.

I knew both Monsignor Dobbin and Father Foster and I had never been a strong partisan of either. Besides I happened to know that "Batten Brothers" was the best firm in the business. I made an independent although tentative decision in favor of "BB."

Musing late at night in my room, I became convinced that my energies should first be devoted toward building up the spiritual life of the parish. The societies would have to be revitalized. Liturgical participation ought to be encouraged.

Some new approaches might be effective. Surely there were many men and women of learning and talent in the parish. A superior type of study club or forum might win many adherents even despite outside attractions. "Superior" was the magnetic word here. The possibility of richly tapestried theological lectures did not seem too fanciful. I had friends on the faculty of the seminary; college professors were traditionally available for paid lectures. No doubt my parishioners included several university scholars.

I grew enthusiastic about my scheme and smoked my pipe wildly for the better part of two hours. As a result I had a slight heart palpitation when I lay down on my bed, and I could not sleep.

The "plan" rolled over and over in my mind as I lay there with my fists clenched and my legs stiff. I wanted to be up and working at once.

I rose but did no work. Instead I listened to an absurd radio program presented by a panel of "experts" on mental telepathy, ghosts, and similar "mystical" phenomena. I decided that I would work out my spiritual program on the morrow with Fathers Mutch and Kingsley. The building program would have to wait a year or so — the Bishop could be persuaded — until a proper parish spirit had been established. After all, I was a pastor of souls not of church buildings and fund-raising associations, although in my midnight canniness, I realized that the building drive would be much more successful if the spiritual integration of the people was effected first. From every aspect my approach seemed ideal.

At last the palpitations and the discussion of "mystical" phenomena subsided, and I returned to my bed for a night of tense and tortured sleep.

My assistants listened patiently to my proposals at lunch the next day. They were, I thought, unduly quiet. I had the impression of determined toleration on their part.

I pressed my point, harder perhaps than was required.

"Excellence," I said. "Excellence, superior performance is the key. We must have a first-rate choir, first-rate appurtenances on the altar. All our services, ceremonies, novenas must be of high quality. I'll ask you to give special attention to your sermons; I'll do the same. We must not only preach well but we must raise the tone, the intellectual content. When we establish a study group, we must enlist the best minds in the parish. Our guest lecturers must be not merely good but at the top in their fields. Our societies must have carefully worked out, challenging programs that will attract really dedicated people. Numbers are not so important at first. If we start with quality, quantity will follow."

I paused for breath, mildly amazed at my own eloquence. It was clear that I was already inspired by my plans.

Father Mutch merely inquired, "You remember what we told you — about our past experiences here?"

"I remember, but we can't abandon noble and necessary objectives because of temporary or partial failures."

"O.K., O.K., I just wanted to be sure you realized the obstacles. We'll do what we can. Eh, Joe?"

Joe Kingsley looked gravely at the wax centerpiece for a while. He could rarely agree completely with any proposition.

At last: "I have some uneasiness about the probable results, or rather the lack thereof. *De jure*, Father, you are undoubtedly about to follow the proper course. But *de facto* the efficiency of your program is likely to be somewhat, if not largely, disappointing. Still I like your *de jure* position, and I will do my best to bring about a *de facto* situation in the parish in keeping with the mind of the Church. I'll give a bit of thought to some possible leaders of the study group."

Our procedures were carefully drawn up in the next few weeks. Father Mutch was to have charge of the liturgical program and Father Kingsley of the intellectual phase. Between them, with help from me in every area, they would attempt to reactivate the traditional Church societies. One of the Brothers in the school already had an active youth group; hence there was no problem there.

The preparatory stage included both theoretical study and direct inspection of successful ventures in other parishes. Within six weeks, we were ready to introduce our leaven into the mass of parishioners of St. Ansgar's. I had explained our plan in a long interview with the Bishop and he had agreed to the postponement of our building drive for two years — provided I filled in the wall cracks and re-enforced the stairs without delay. This I agreed to do since the parish had sufficient funds already on deposit. I thought the Bishop looked at me somewhat admiringly as I departed, but perhaps this was only my resurgent vanity.

The liturgical effort, after a modest beginning, gathered great momentum. Communions, I dare say, increased by one fourth in the first year, and when we scheduled a noontide Mass, we had nearly half a church daily. It is true that Vespers on Sunday evenings drew only a faithful hard core, but the Solemn High Mass at 10 a.m. was well attended and more than one parishioner, flushed with the beauty of it, told us that our choir's singing could well rival that of the Cathedral's famed choristers. It took a great deal of letter-writing, telephoning, and high-pressure persuasion on my part to induce the best preachers in the metropolitan area to come to our aid, but in this I had eventual success. On one or two occasions, I even imported men from the Midwest. There was a small but noticeable increase in attendance at novenas and Lenten courses, and we felt well repaid for our efforts. Our special pride was the Missa Recitata on Sundays in which the people recited many of the prayers.

The societies had a 10 per cent increase both in numbers and in tone, but I was not satisfied with this. I made it a subject for sermonizing, becoming deep and theological in my explanations as to why the matrons of the parish should take an active part in the Rosary Society.

The study club seemed to be one of the most successful aspects of our program and I rarely failed to take my place in the back of the hall to hear the discussions on philosophical and theological questions. Father Kingsley had been fortunate in interesting several young intellectuals, including professors and periodical writers, and they in turn had gathered around them an enthusiastic group of college students and recent college graduates — mostly female, although there were a few bespectacled males among them. They held open discussions on such subjects as "The Postulates of a Pluralistic Society," "The Coming Catholic-Protestant Dialogue," and "Communication in the Postwar World." Their ideas seemed remarkably deep and advanced and they quoted freely from philosophers and theologians of whom I had heard only vaguely or not at all. The names of Mounier, Marcel, and Buber were frequently mentioned; all these men seemed to see the salvation of the modern world in some special sort of communion or communication between human beings in a spirit of what I presumed to be Christian charity. It was never entirely clear to me what was new in this doctrine, for it seemed as old as Christianity, but it made for fine talk and many new terms such as "openness," "I and thou relationship," and "reciprocal presence," which were frequently used with great feeling. One of the professors, Panella, a dark-haired vivacious young man, never lost an opportunity to stress the importance of putting the age-old truths in the modern idiom. In a sense he dominated the meetings, and the young women always gathered around him enthusiastically when the coffee was served at the end. There were several other young men, however, who also spoke brilliantly, but there was rarely any serious disagreement among them. Panella's ideas were almost universally endorsed. I say "almost," because there was a man named Campbell who surprised many by his vigorous opposition as time went on.

He was a balding, stocky man of about thirty-five with

an incipient corporation which his double-breasted suits were not entirely able to conceal. He spoke in a distinct but slightly diffident tone which might easily have led a listener to underestimate his intellectual ability. He was in fact the brightest and the best educated man in the group although his ideas were so poorly received by the majority of those present that you might at times have thought that he was an intellectual eccentric. As a matter of fact, I soon discovered that he was precisely orthodox in his statements and usually had much more solid theological opinion in his favor than anyone else.

Even I, who had at first been tolerantly fascinated by the novel views of Panella and his group, began to grow alarmed after about four months. It seemed to me that statements were being made which were rather daring and even wild when compared with my own knowledge of theology. I attributed this to my own intellectual rustiness at first, then to the youthful enthusiasm of the participants, but finally I was led to suspect that several of our young intellectuals were either not well grounded in philosophy and theology or else they were deliberately making statements beyond the bounds of orthodoxy. Of course they always threw in a saving phrase or a sentence which seemed to exorcise heresy, but their emphasis, it seemed to me, was often decidedly dangerous. Campbell always rose to correct their errors, but they usually had some clerical author (whose name was unfamiliar to me) to justify their position, and they laughingly passed off Campbell's strictures as the result of "integralist" training. Although I was growing more and more worried as time went on, I was hesitant to interfere because I feared that the study group would collapse if I assumed the role of "witch-hunter." Father Kingsley, I knew, felt that if any corrections were to be made, it should be my responsibility since I attended all the meetings. I found myself forced to renew my studies and, as I did so, I grew more and more convinced that Panella and his clique were making some statements and advocating some positions which were well beyond what competent theologians would allow.

I remember especially the fatal meeting just before the beginning of Lent.

As usual about fifty men and women were gathered in the front seats of the large, brightly lighted auditorium. A cloud of tobacco smoke hung over them as they listened to Dr. Panella, who was seated at a wooden table, concluding his paper on the new trends in theology.

"The restrictive, integralist atmosphere of the Vatican Council," he intoned in his full rich voice, "and of its succeeding generation has now largely been dissipated by the efforts of those who have worked persistently within the Church to re-evaluate Christian attitudes in the light of modern technology, modern problems, and modern thought. There is no question here of modernist heresy but of re-leasing the inner riches of Christian dogma and spirituality which have been too long pent up by ultraconservative thinkers who have failed to recognize the dynamic and adaptive potentialities of the treasury of faith and grace. The recent stir and movement in Christian thinking both within and without the pale of the Church are a basis for an appeal to modern man such as has not been possible in the entire post-Tridentine and especially in the post-Vatican Council era. The narrow theology which so long succeeded in stultifying Catholic thought with the illusion that the last word on Divine Truth had been written long ago has now been given the lie. We can approach our Protestant brethren in an idiom which they can understand and with a re-examination of age-old doctrines which cannot help winning their sincere interest. The modern Catholic scholar, having thrown away the obsolete weapons of death-dealing polemics, will approach his confreres on the other side of the line with the life-giving formulations of a Truth that

201

is indeed eternally vital and now, more than ever, free of the oppressive habiliments of medieval verbalisms. And our approach will be one of great humility, with our spirits contrite at the ghettolike irresponsibility of much of Catholic thought in past decades and appreciative of the accomplishments of the many non-Catholic thinkers whose enlightened probings into our own heritage have at last wakened us from our sterile complacency."

The applause seemed endless. Panella looked modestly down at his notes. His slightly flushed cheeks were the only sign that he was moved by his success. The cloud of smoke grew thicker and thicker.

His words were ringing in my ears, but I was not happy. His remarks had been vague enough to evade the strict pin-pointing of error, but I could smell heresy somewhere in their implications.

"This guy is way out of line," I croaked to Father Kingsley who was sitting rigidly beside me.

"I know now why the Pope wrote *Humani Generis*," he replied. "But this lad has some French theologians on his side. I've talked to him in private and he backs away from anything specifically erroneous, and he can always quote some European priest to back up his vague generalities."

"I think we'll have to get him quietly out of the way or the whole parish will be under interdict," I said.

"If he goes, the whole study club goes smash, except for Campbell and a few others. He has most of these people hypnotized."

"Then we'll have to discredit him openly," I said. "In that way he'll lose his ascendancy. If we could just catch him in a few clear-cut, specific statements contrary to official Church teaching, then we could destroy his hold on these young people."

Father Kingsley shook his head. "He's too clever for that. He knows how to back and dodge, and he's an expert at vague implications. I think the only solution is to ring down the curtain on the whole enterprise."

"I'll have to think it through," I said.

There was some discussion going on in the front. Familiar phrases like "pluralistic society" and "outmoded paternalism" floated back along the length of the hall. Then I heard the diffident drawl of Campbell and I immediately sharpened my attention. Here might be our solution. If we gave the balding writer enough ammunition he might be able to perform successfully the role of executioner. Or was I, too, a victim of the narrow post-Tridentine disease of polemicism?

"I don't know if you're aware of it, Dr. Panella," Campbell was saying, "but His Holiness has recently issued an encyclical *Humani Generis* which has some very interesting comments on the loose ideas and the unorthodox vocabulary of so-called 'New Theology.' It seems clear from what he says that certain European theologians have stepped far out of bounds in their efforts to distort Catholic teaching to so-called modern needs under the guise of doing away with the alleged 'oppressive habiliments of medieval verbalisms' as you call them. We can't alter divine truth to satisfy non-Catholics and neopagans, and you'll pardon me if I say that I think some of the remarks which you have just made seem to smack of the very thing the Pope condemned. It's one thing to apply immutable principles to new problems and situations; it's another matter to imply, however subtly, that the principles themselves need changing. That's where the Modernists went off around the turn of the century, and there seems to be a resurgent Modernism in the air today. I mean no offense, but I feel that some of the things you said are confusing, vague, and potentially dangerous to a group like this. I think we ought to stick to studying the clear and definite teaching of the Church when we discuss theology and not go off on questionable tangents and dubious lines of thought which may be harmful to us all."

Panella stood up at his table — tense, flushed, threatening. Then he sat down again with a strangled laugh.

"O.K., Bob," he said, "call me a heretic if you wish, but I can name at least three first-class theologians who say in their books and articles exactly what I've said, and they put it even more strongly. I don't get my ideas out of the air, you know. But I must say I hardly expected to meet an integralist in a group like this. The integralists went witch-hunting after every writer of their day who offered a fresh approach to theological questions. Many a so-called 'modernist' was black-listed or hounded out of the Church by these self-appointed vigilantes. Yes, I'm not afraid to say it, because it's been said by competent Church scholars, that a lot of alleged modernists were made to appear a lot worse than they were by these narrow-minded defenders of the Faith. The same, apparently, is going to be true today. I've read and studied *Humani Generis* and I know that the Pope doesn't name a single name in it. And I also know that there's not a single thing I've said that is in any way opposed to the Holy Father's statements. There may have been a few French thinkers who went a little too far in their tentative theses, but certainly the Pope doesn't intend to kill the fresh initiative in theology and the up-to-date developments of truths too long buried in the deposit of Faith. I resent the implication that I'm somehow unorthodox when my deepest desire is to make Catholic doctrine understandable in the modern context and dynamic in modern living. I think you owe me, all of us, an apology, Bob."

Panella's speech was delivered in an intense, sincere, slightly aggrieved tone that was very impressive. The applause was loud and long.

"I'm sorry if I hurt anybody's feelings," Campbell replied, very slowly, very distinctly, "and I had no intention of accusing anyone of heresy. I merely say that in view of the Pope's encyclical, I think a group like this should stay within safe boundaries. Let the experts settle the dubious areas; there's enough clear and definite teaching for us to explore without running the risk of going out of bounds."

"I'm sorry, Bob, but that's an approach I can't see. We're mid-twentieth-century Catholics interested in mid-twentieth-century problems. We ought to look for the best and most satisfactory answers we can find in the mid-twentieth-century context."

Panella hesitated for a moment and stared at the table. Then he looked up and fixed his eyes on the ceiling.

"Since you emphasize *Humani Generis* so much, we should of course note first that this is not an infallible document, and secondly that, according to some reports, the Pope was euchred into writing it by a group of Roman integralists who are envious of the brilliance of the French school. This may or may not be true but the rumor is going around in academic circles."

Immediately I was on my feet, choking, trying to speak but unable to find words.

Father Kingsley pulled me down. "Later," he whispered hoarsely, "later! Now is not the time — too much scandal. Later you can handle him."

Breathing heavily, I tried to relax. I hadn't been so angry in years. My heart was beating wildly. I did not hear what else was said. Fortunately the meeting ended quickly. As I climbed the stairs slowly to my room, I was feeling really sick. It was the pounding of the heart which bothered me most.

The next day I went to Dr. Parks's office and submitted to a half hour's intensive examination.

"You're relatively fit," the lean little doctor commented at the end. "Put on your shirt; you're not going to die yet. Your heart is taking some extra beats now and again, but I can detect no real ailment. A lot of people have that type of stimulation as a result of exercise, smoking, emotion —

even fatigue. It comes and goes and doesn't mean a thing. Cut down on your smoking and don't get too excited about anything, and it won't bother you so much. Now get out of here so I can attend to some really sick people."

I walked back to the rectory pleased but a little skeptical. Why hadn't he at least prescribed a cardiogram? I smoked only a pipe and I wasn't any more excitable than anyone else — less if anything. It was true that I had been feeling more tired than usual lately. But it was a matter of slight degree. I had been tired all my adult life.

I sat in my room and read the afternoon paper without conscious awareness of a single item. There was one all-pervasive problem inhabiting my mind. Should I call Panella in, or not? My moment of truth came at last. This was my problem, not Campbell's, not even Father Kingsley's. I had evaded responsibility at Royalton, with tragic consequences. Even though it would mean another night of palpitations, I would have to bring Panella to heel. As I picked up the phone, I realized that my heart was already hammering.

Meekly and without apparent surprise, he said that he would come right over. I had been hoping for a nap, for dinner, for time to prepare myself emotionally, but he said that he would not be available in the evening.

"I'll see you then in a few minutes," I said, my voice strange and unsteady.

I met him at the door with a forced smile and led him into the small office. Without waiting for my request, he closed the door behind him.

"Sit down, Dr. Panella. I thought I ought to talk to you about last night — not just last night actually, but about a general impression, if you know what I mean."

He pulled out a pouch. "May I smoke?"

"Certainly." Smoking was against our office rules, but I had to make some concessions in view of what I was going to say.

He lighted the huge pipe and sat back comfortably in the uncomfortable chair.

He shook his head innocently. "Perhaps you'd better explain just what you mean, Father."

His tone seemed slightly arrogant but I was not going to grow angry.

"I refer to some of the remarks you made last night and also on previous occasions. I don't want to offend you, Dr. Panella, but I think that a number of your statements on theological matters could easily be a source of confusion to the young men and women in our study club. I understand that you are trying to challenge your listeners, but they could easily misinterpret what you say. In fact, even allowing for all possible implied qualifications, I must admit that I do not see how some things you have said can be squared with the official teaching of the Church."

"Could you perhaps be more specific? Could you indicate one such statement?"

"You definitely implied last night that two great popes were tricked into invalid condemnations, Pope Pius X into condemning modernism and Pope Pius XII into denouncing the so-called 'New Theology.'"

He leaned forward stiffly, his dark eyes filled with intensity. "I implied, Father? Is that fair? I mentioned neither pope by name, and in fact I implied, if anything, that some in the groups condemned had gone to extremes. I advocated nothing really unorthodox, nothing that can't be found in books and magazines written with ecclesiastical approval. I did mention that there was a rumor that undue influence had been used on the present Holy Father, but it was clear that I was merely reporting hearsay statements and that I did not necessarily endorse this view myself. But even if I had endorsed it, is this heretical? Isn't it realistic to suppose that the Pope does not write his encyclicals and other allocutions out of thin air, that he has men around him who persuade him to act in this or that matter, to follow a certain line of thought? Surely these are not infallible documents."

"Perhaps not," I said, "but they represent the official teaching of the Church. We cannot discount the Pope's statements on the grounds that they may have been suggested to him by his advisers. We must believe that he takes all points of view into account, and especially the traditional teaching of the Church before he composes his utterances. Furthermore we must hold that he is guided by the grace of his office even in his noninfallible writings."

I could feel the blood in my cheeks and a dull pounding in my chest, but I was more confident than I would have believed possible. I was surprised at my own fluency.

"Once we admit the type of attitude embodied in your remarks, Dr. Panella where do we draw the line? It would seem to follow that we could brush aside all papal pronouncements, not specifically *ex cathedra,* as having been inspired by partisan groups surrounding the Pope. The fact of the matter is, Dr. Panella, that all the Pontiff's pronouncements on faith and morals are binding upon all Catholics in virtue of his teaching authority and we must accept them as authoritative, infallible or not."

His jaw hung down for a significant moment and his eyes seemed glazed. Then he recovered.

"I think you're pressing a good point a little too far, Father."

I knew what I knew. "The youngest student in the seminary is aware of the truth of what I've said, Dr. Panella. I'm surprised that this elementary point has escaped you. In fact a restatement of it is contained in the very encyclical we were discussing, *Humani Generis.*"

"I see." He spoke slowly. "Well, of course, I never had any intention of impugning the Pope's teaching — far from it. In fact I am interested in bringing the riches of the

Church's wisdom to bear on the modern condition."

His voice gained confidence. "I want you to know, Father, that I am a loyal son of the Church."

"I don't doubt that," I replied. I tried to smile but my facial muscles trembled badly. "I simply wanted to point out to you the imprudence of the approach you are using in your talks at the study club, especially when you consider that these young people are not trained theologians and have no well-grounded basis from which to evaluate your remarks. Young people tend to jump at novelties. Why give them dubious or, at best, untested theories in theology when there are so many solid doctrinal points with which they're not as well acquainted as they should be? I think our study club should concentrate on the latter, Dr. Panella, and I can't agree with you that these things are remote from the 'modern condition,' as you term it. I'd like your assurance that you'll stick to the safe path in your future utterances within the club."

I felt almost ashamed of myself as I made this demand. After all, I had always thought of myself as a middle-of-the-roader in theology. In legitimately disputed matters, I had never leaned to the more rigid view. Now it appeared that I had assumed an overrigid role. At least it seemed to me that I could read this opinion in Dr. Panella's narrowing eyes.

He stood up suddenly and held out his hand. There was an enigmatic smile around his mouth although his eyes were hurt and serious.

"I assure you, Father," he said slowly, "you will have no need to worry about my future utterances in the club."

With a sense of defeat in victory, I escorted him in silence to the door. . . .

He never returned to the study club although he remained in the parish, for I saw him frequently at the Communion rail. We lost half our club members but the group which persevered was faithful and interested in the pursuit of solid doctrine. All in all, I felt, and my assistants agreed with me, that I had acted prudently. Nevertheless, I would have wished Dr. Panella and his party to remain.

After a year and a half, when my spiritual program was running smoothly, I felt it was time to call in the fund-raising group. I must admit that they were far more efficient in their field than I was in mine. In the space of a few weeks they had raised ten thousand dollars more than we had hoped for. The parish hummed with co-operation and a new spirit of loyalty seemed to be in the air. Consequently, I was only slightly surprised when we received a pledge of five hundred dollars from the unorthodox Dr. Panella.

You can visualize without my help the dedication of the new rectory, with the crowds of priests and altar boys and parishioners and of course the Bishop. There were the usual ceremonies and the speeches, and the refreshments. I need not analyze my mixed emotions when His Excellency announced that the Holy Father had conferred upon me the title of Right Reverend Monsignor. These occurrences are too well known to need detail.

It was just too bad that I should have had my heart attack that same night as I prepared for bed, but then, if I had not been stricken, I would not have had the opportunity to write this story of the more unusual events of a priestly life that has been on the whole routine and unexceptional and, I regret to say, much less effective than I would have hoped. But I am thankful to God for having given me so many opportunities for good in so many places, even though I have not used these opportunities well, even though sometimes I think wistfully that I could have done better work if He had left me, like the Curé d'Ars, for a lifetime in one place among the same people, whom I might have learned to love and who possibly would have learned to love me as time went on.